The Bloody Wood

The Bloody Wood

MICHAEL INNES

Dodd, Mead & Company

NEW YORK

Published by Dodd, Mead & Company, Inc.
79 Madison Avenue, New York, N.Y. 10016

Distributed in Canada by
McClelland and Stewart Limited, Toronto

Manufactured in the United States of America

First Red Badge printing

Library of Congress Catalog Card Number: 66-14192
ISBN: 0-396-08238-6

Contents

PART ONE

Husband and Wife

. . . And sang within the bloody wood
When Agamemnon cried aloud,
And let their liquid siftings fall
To stain the stiff dishonoured shroud.

T. S. Eliot
Sweeney Among the Nightingales

Chapter 1

"Do NIGHTINGALES eat apples?" Bobby Angrave asked idly. He was a small, dark and handsome youth, in his second year at Oxford.

"Why should they be supposed to?" Stirred to interest, Mrs. Martineau leaned forward in her enveloping shawl. Her eyes, glittering in the near darkness, seemed to light up the waxen skin which was drawn so fearfully tight over her beautifully modelled face.

"It's the meaning of the Greek word, more or less. Philomel—lover of the apple."

"I thought," Charles Martineau said, "that it meant lover of melody. Isn't there a little poem? 'Philomel, with melody, Sing in our sweet lullaby'—something like that." He spoke absently. Like his wife, he was listening for the next burst of song from the wood.

"Perhaps it does. But take it that way and you're in trouble between μέλος and μῆλον. You have to suppose some lengthening of the vowel."

A moment's silence followed this learned communication by Bobby. He had lately taken a First in Classical Moderations, and was understood to be devoting this

3

part of his vacation—dutifully spent with his uncle and aunt—to the composition of a prize poem in some ancient language. Bobby was undoubtedly very clever.

"And still they gaz'd, and still the wonder grew,
That one small head could carry all he knew."

It was Diana Page who had broken the silence with this. It appeared to be her role to tease Bobby Angrave. But this time—or so Sir John Appleby thought, as he studied what could be distinguished of the company in the dusk—she had come up with her joke a little belatedly. The child—for Diana could be no more than eighteen or nineteen—was for some reason less than happy. Of course there was constraint abroad in the place. Their hostess, Grace Martineau, was very ill; she had passed beyond the point at which a woman might be expected to summon even a small and intimate house party around her. And the young do not take kindly to the spectacle of human dissolution. Perhaps it was nothing more than this that accounted for the glint of something like panic in Diana. And Diana was the greatest stranger present. She was here simply as the friend of Martine Rivière, Grace Martineau's favourite niece.

"There!" Martine said softly.

From the heart of the wood the tremendous song was rising again. *Eternal passion*—Appleby thought—*eternal pain.*

Charne was a plain four-square Georgian house— about the right size, as Judith Appleby put it, for a Jane Austen baronet of ten thousand a year. Charles Martineau, although not a baronet, had presumably a good

4

deal more than that. Martineaus had lived at Charne for generations, but Charles was the first of them to have slipped out into the world and brought back a fortune, as fortunes now go. The fortune wasn't made greatly to appear—although when one took a good look round, one saw that everything was unobtrusively perfect. Judith Appleby liked coming to Charne. Her people, the Ravens, held some sort of relationship with the Martineaus, as they seemed to do with a lot of people of the same sort. Charles Martineau commonly called her "cousin Judith"—a form of address which was surely coming to take on an old-fashioned air. John Appleby, who hadn't been bred to such places, liked coming to Charne too. This was chiefly because he liked Martineau. He seemed so utterly gentle a man that the fortune he had made presented itself as a puzzle. It is usually rather tough characters who come by anything of that sort. Perhaps Charles's nature changed when he left Charne behind him.

"Do nightingales sing only at night?" Diana asked "Poems and things make it seem like that."

"Hark, from that moonlit cedar what a burst!" Bobby Angrave produced this with a faintly ironical effect. It was a quotation, Appleby reflected, from the poem that had been running in his own head. *Again—thou hearest! Eternal Passion! Eternal Pain!*

"No, my dear." Mrs. Martineau seemed almost shocked by Diana's ignorance. "Where there are nightingales, and one listens carefully, one may hear their notes all through an afternoon."

"But it's in the evening that they rev up," Martine said.

5

"That is true. And the other birds make so much noise by day. This nightingale—our nightingale—we have heard only by night."

"O Nightingale, that on yon bloomy Spray
Warbl'st at eve, when all the woods are still."

This was Bobby again, and it ought to have been harmless and agreeable. But it wasn't, Appleby thought—or not quite. Grace Martineau could be sensed as stiffening in displeasure as if she felt Bobby—her husband's nephew—to be guying this new poem, and so guying the bird. And it was quite possible—one suddenly perceived —that Grace didn't much like Bobby, anyway.

And Diana Page, too, seemed not pleased, for she launched another attack on the young man.

"Fancy spouting poetry about the nightingale," she said, "when one can sit still and listen to it! And it isn't even difficult. Anybody could go on producing nightingales till bedtime."

"Try," Bobby said. He seemed nettled by this juvenile assault.

"Still are thy pleasant voices, the nightingales, awake."

"Try again."

"Thou wast not born for death, immortal bird."

"And again." Bobby was now mocking.

There was a moment's silence, as Diana hesitated. Mrs. Martineau, barely visible, made a faint gesture of displeasure.

"He sings each song twice over," Diana said, "lest you should think—"

Bobby interrupted with a shout of laughter—a sound too loud for the hour and place.

"You silly goose," he said, "that's the thrush."

"Well, I think it's true of the nightingale as well. This one has sung tonight exactly as he sang last night. So there!"

Bobby Angrave stood up—deftly capturing, in face of this apology for an argument, the air of one who tactfully breaks off conference with a petulant child.

"I think I'll go and have a chat with the bird," he said. And he strolled off into the darkness.

There was another burst of song, to which they listened in silence. The nightingale seemed to have its station at some distance from the house. The glazed loggia in which they were sitting had been added to the east pavilion—one of two small Palladian structures which served to modify the cubelike severity of the house. In front of them—which was to the south—lay a broad terrace beyond the balustrade of which the ground dropped down shallow flights of steps to the ghost of a formal garden. You could see—or in daylight you could see—the outlines of intricately patterned flower beds. Now, except for two great stone basins—and these were dry—the whole space was grassed over. It wasn't untended; it had merely been thus simplified, you guessed, as the consequence of some instinct on Charles Martineau's part to seek out the spirit of the time. It wasn't possible to doubt that he could have had gardeners working about the place by the score. Indeed, you saw as you strolled plenty of evidence of activities beyond the scope of, say, an old man and a boy. But the immediate prospect from the front of the house was like this. If you looked down from an upper window, the forsaken garden might have suggested the obscure activities of prehistoric men, which the

7

passing of millennia had all but obliterated. But perhaps it was designed to speak rather of the future. It was what Charne, a proud and elegant façade, was fronting and sailing into. That, roughly speaking, might be the idea. It wasn't very obtrusively asserted. The great expanse of grass, if not shorn, was controlled by expensive machines. There were gravel paths, so that in walking around you would be as secure as the baronet's wife and daughters would have been against getting your feet wet. If you peered, it would probably be to see that the gravel was very nicely raked.

All this was now fading in the summer dusk. To the east and north the wood curved round the house at only a near remove, and this was where the nightingale sang. You could climb through the wood by various paths to higher ground—passing here and there across a glade which in spring would be a sea of bluebells, and here and there beneath enormous senatorial oaks which had been part of a great forest once. There was a belvedere that looked down a long grassy ride into a vista closed by a church tower. There were several cavelike places, decked out in the eighteenth century as grottoes with shellwork and curiously eroded stones—retreats, you had to suppose, in the height of summers fiercer than ours. There was a spring, issuing from a rocky outcrop much embellished in the same age with tritons, dolphins and urns, from which a stream ran gently downhill and through a succession of small, deep pools upon whose surface the water-lily leaves were never quite still. In the wood, in fact—as Appleby vulgarly put it to himself—you had all the works. But everything was contained in no great space, you would find upon more careful survey. Go through the wood, and in no time you were in the village. And the village was now no more than the fringe of the town. The town was creeping round Charne. Still just held invisible, it was nevertheless biding its time to strangle the place.

Appleby thought of Grace Martineau, a sick woman swathed in shawls, waiting too.

"Perhaps we should move indoors?" Charles Martineau said. He spoke—carefully—not to his wife, but to the company at large. "It turns chilly. And there may be damp in the air."

Martineau had nothing of the hypochondriac about him. The notion of damp in the air was not one that would come to him naturally. He must live at present, Appleby thought, submerged in anxious care, knowing himself on the verge of loss.

"No, Charles," Grace Martineau replied before any of her guests could. "Let us stay a little longer. This place keeps the warmth of the sun. And we must hear the nightingale once more."

"Yes, of course. But would you be the better of a rug? Shall I ring for Friary on this telephone?"

Mrs. Martineau had turned on a low light. She could be seen to look at her watch.

"But, Charles, it is Friary's hour for his little walk."

"So it is. But the telephone won't go unanswered because of that, you know. Perhaps—"

"I am quite warm. I am quite comfortable." The pitch of Mrs. Martineau's voice had risen a little, so that for a moment her comfort was scarcely shared by her guests. But of this she seemed at once to be aware, for she signed to Judith Appleby to take a seat closer to her, and began to speak on a relaxed note. "Do you know," she said, "about Friary's being like a clock?"

"I know that everything is always very punctually conducted at Charne. And when things are like that, I suppose it is the butler who is responsible."

"Yes—but I am thinking of this little evening walk of his. It is something about which Charles is very indulgent; he says that an evening walk ought to be within the command of anybody who sees it as a rational pleasure."

"Is that how Friary sees it?"

"My dear Judith, I don't think I could swear to that. Friary dresses for it a little too fashionably. That is to say, he puts on a well-cut dustcoat over what we may call his professional attire, and makes his way through the wood to the village. I think he goes to the Charne Arms, but no doubt he is conscious of the beauties of nature on the way."

"That is what we like to think," Charles Martineau said. He seemed to be catching hopefully at some shift in his wife's mood. "It is certainly why I sanction this regular withdrawal at an hour at which butlers are commonly required to buttle."

"I think it very nice of you," Judith said. "It's not as if Friary can be regarded as in a category of indulged because ancient retainers. He's surprisingly young. And he's good-looking, too."

"Ah—I see the direction in which your mind is moving." Charles Martineau glanced at his wife, and laughed quite gaily. "It appears very likely that Friary may have affairs of the heart in the village. But we prefer to suppose—just to avoid anxious thoughts—that the sole purpose of his vespertine pilgrimage is brief relaxation within some favoured circle of superior habitués in the village pub."

"And if he is a wooer," Grace Martineau said, "he is certainly a brisk one. I've never known him not be back in the music room before anybody's bedtime, and very much in command of his decanters and syphons."

"He comes back through the wood?" Judith asked.

"Oh, certainly. It is what I was going to say. You know the little belvedere? Well, I must confess to an absurd habit, if Charles will let me. Charles, may I tell?"

"You may." Charles Martineau leaned forward and lightly touched his wife's hand where it lay, emaciated and fine-boned, on the arm of her chair. It was a gesture too unself-consciously tender to be embarrassing.

"It was our favourite place in the grounds in the early days of our marriage. We used to sit in it of an evening and gossip famously—about our reading, and the improvements we were going to carry out at Charne, and all our neighbours for thirty miles around. They were quite new to me, for the most part, because I had been brought up in another county."

"The belvedere was just the right place." Appleby, perhaps because amused by this last territorial touch, put in this cheerfully. "Seclusion—and at the same time a marvellous vista."

"Yes." Mrs. Martineau smiled with pleasure, and nodded gently. Whatever county she had been bred in, it was evident that her present part of this one was very dear to her. "Well, we have been taking, Charles and I, to going there again sometimes, just at about this time in the evening. You must none of you be offended if we vanish, perhaps tomorrow evening, perhaps the evening after.

You will at least be in our thoughts."

"Grace means," Charles Martineau said, "that we shall be gossiping about you all quite shamelessly."

"As soon, that is, as we have got our breath—for the climb is a little hard. And it is only Friary who will stop us."

"Friary has instructions?" Judith asked.

"Oh, no. We like to think he knows nothing about it. But we see him pass—quite close by—and so punctually that it is like having a clock in the belvedere. Which is what I was saying when I started rambling. And then, you see, we come away, Charles and I. Usually together, but sometimes first one and then the other. For we like to show that we can be a little independent of each other still."

Grace Martineau stopped speaking—and upon her last words there succeeded a silence it might not have been easy to break. Tactfully, the nightingale ended it with another burst of song. They listened until there came a pause.

"You know, until quite lately, we used to have king-fishers by the stream." Mrs. Martineau spoke, this time, in a low voice, as if for Judith Appleby's ear alone. "I am afraid we shan't see them again. But the nightingales have come back, as I have longed for them to do." She leaned forward, and touched Judith's arm. "There . . . you see?"

On one of the grassy paths issuing from the wood there had appeared the figure of Friary. His coat could certainly be distinguished as sitting well on him. He moved briskly and with a light tread. He might have been a son of the house, Appleby thought, who had been out

12

and about some necessary business on the estate. One rather expected a hail from him or a casual wave.

But, of course, nothing of the sort occurred. With his gaze decorously averted from his distant employers and their guests, Friary turned right, and disappeared round the back of the house.

Chapter 2

THE NIGHTINGALE had ceased, and somewhere in the wood an owl was hooting, as if issuing a challenge to one of those feathered *débats* or wordy wrangles so tediously reported by mediaeval poets. If so, the nightingale was not taking it on, but now remained obstinately mute. One had to suppose that, belying its reputation for nightlong activity, it had tucked its head under its wing and gone to sleep.

This might have been judged the more perverse in the nightingale in that the setting was steadily becoming apter for the exhibition of its prowess. The moon had risen behind the wood, and in the park which lay beyond the forsaken garden not one but half a dozen moonlit cedars were invitingly untenanted. But only the owl hooted again; it was possible to hear a faint plash of water from the stream; it was possible to imagine that one heard, fainter still, a murmur which might have come from waves on a distant beach, but that in fact must come—if indeed it was there at all—from the encroaching city. And into the sky the city cast a dull red glow which the moonlight was now engaged in combating. Charne was a wholly manmade place; within sight of the house nothing more than an occasional weed or shrub or small sapling grew where it hadn't been told to. Yet everything was sufficiently mature to approximate it to the order of nature—and this order the moonlight might now be felt as championing. It was with a sense of victory that one watched the hot red glare of urban life beaten back on the eastern sky. And already, except in shadowed places, it would be possible to see one's footing clearly. Appleby, marking this, felt the attraction of the night. He was about to get up and stroll away, when Mrs. Martineau broke the silence.

"I am afraid I took no part in your game," she said. Her voice held a note of apology. "You must forgive me. My thoughts sometimes go far away."

"Our game, Grace?" It had been after a baffled moment that Charles Martineau said this questioningly.

"Remembering what the poets have said about the nightingale."

"Yes, of course." Judith Appleby said this. She had not spoken for some time. "Bobby and Diana were playing a game like that."

"And now I recall something I could have joined in with." Mrs. Martineau's voice could just be heard. Her strength nowadays seemed to come and go, and at times seemed barely sufficient for articulate speech. "I think it is from Keats," she said. "Didn't somebody quote from Keats?"

"I did," Diana said. "Before I got snubbed. It was the bit about 'immortal bird.' I know that was right, because we did it at school. Keats wrote a whole poem just about a nightingale, didn't he?"

"Yes, dear, I think he did." Mrs. Martineau spoke indulgently—as nearly everybody except Bobby Angrave did to Diana, who was undeniably not clever. "Only, my lines don't come from that poem. I'm not sure where they come from."

There was a moment's pause. For some obscure reason, nobody seemed eager to prompt Mrs. Martineau to go on. But presently she did so of her own accord—and so quietly that she somehow gave no effect of quoting verse.

"It is a flaw in happiness," Mrs. Martineau said, "to see beyond our bourne. It forces us in summer nights to mourn. It spoils the singing of the nightingale."

This produced silence. It was a silence lasting until Diana spoke again—and with all the rashness of ignorance.

"What's a bourne?" Diana asked.

"Well, dear, it can be several things, I believe. For another of the poets, Shakespeare, it is that from which no traveller returns."

"Uncle Charles, I think I heard a car. Are we going to have visitors?" Martine Rivière, a girl at once alert and curiously withdrawn, plunged into the talk. It was reasonable that she should feel diversion to be required hard upon her aunt's having relapsed upon so uncomfortably sombre a note. But she hadn't, as it turned out, chosen too well.

"It must be Fell." Charles Martineau's voice was barely steady. "He has formed the habit of dropping in of an evening. It's on his way home—after doing a late round."

Gregory Fell, Appleby remembered, was the Marti-

16

neaus' family doctor. He was a comparative newcomer to the district, and said to be a man of great ability. It would have been surprising, perhaps, if he had really become an intimate at Charne in the way that Martineau's words suggested. But nobody was deceived. There was too evident a reason why the doctor should pay this evening visit—and why he should frequently appear at other times as well. Appleby wondered whether it was Martineau or Martineau's wife who insisted upon this paper-thin convention of reticence. If Grace Martineau was to have sleep—it was painfully clear—Dr. Fell must bring it to her.

And now, almost with haste, the little party in the loggia was breaking up. The nightingale, should it think to resume its entertainment, would pour out its incredible strains in vain. Nor would the owl be attended to.

"I think I'll take a stroll in search of Angrave," Appleby said. Almost as if he were as young as Diana Page, he was finding intolerable for a moment the simple fact that somebody was going to die. Or at least he supposed that this was what he was feeling. Certainly he wanted a short spell of solitude before the final ritual assembly in the music room prior to bedtime. "There's sufficient light," he said, "to track the young man down."

"Yes—do go. See what Bobby's up to." Martineau, already on his feet, produced this rather oddly. "But don't, either of you, be long." He paused, and seemed conscious that this was a strange circumscription to lay upon a guest—or upon a guest of Appleby's seniority. "It's turning damp," he said. "It's turning chilly."

"Charles, dear—shall we go in together?" Grace Martineau had stood up unaided, but with effort. With

17

an air as of whimsical formality, she placed herself on her husband's arm. But it was a support nobody could suppose her not to need. Together, husband and wife made their way slowly down the little colonnade joining the pavilion to the house. The others followed, trying to disguise the unnatural slowness of their progress by pausing to draw each other's attention to this or that. Appleby caught his wife's eye—and knew that Judith was asking herself, precisely as he was, whether all this ignoring of the spectre wasn't a kind of madness that only the English can produce. Then he turned away, and walked across the terrace.

It was a perfect night in early June. Dropping down from the level of the house, Appleby wandered for a time in the garden, or ghost of a garden, below. Bobby Angrave wasn't at all on his mind, he found; indeed, he must have mentioned his name merely as an excuse for this quiet prowl. He even thought of making his way to the walled garden to the west of the house, and so ensure himself solitude—for Bobby had appeared to make his way into the wood on the east. But this might convict him of mild disingenuousness if he was questioned later, and for the time being he contented himself with lighting a cigar and strolling up and down where he was.

Here, rather more clearly than in the loggia, one could hear the sound of running water. And here, too, that other and urban murmur from beyond the wood was indubitable. Marshalling yards and the clanking of heavy wagons over points, the miscellaneous traffic of city streets and suburban roads, sounds of industrial activity in factories where night shifts were working: all these went to produce this faint continuum that just touched the ear. Probably it touched the ears of the owls and the nightingales too, and they weren't very happy about it. The owls would hold out longest; any summer, one felt, might be the last in which the nightingales would be guests at Charne. There was already ominous talk of a "development," Appleby had been told, on the other side of the high road near the back of the house. That would finish the place as giving any illusion of rural solitude. What Keats called "the hum of mighty workings" would have got hold, good and proper.

Dipping into the English poets was catching. Nobody had announced that the nightingales were singing round the convent of the Sacred Heart—although in one glade in Charne Wood there was a little artificial ruin that might stand for that: a few broken arches and the like, over which ivy and honeysuckle appropriately climbed. Appleby turned round and gazed at the house. Quite a different impulse had been at work there. It looked uncompromisingly permanent, totally removed from the ravages of time. The impression didn't come merely from its solidity, or even from its being in perfect repair. Its proportions were refined; were, one might say, a kind of mathematics in stone. And mathematics we know to be the one absolutely enduring thing.

But if houses are to remain houses, they must continue to be lived in. Appleby's thought veered from these speculative ruminations into a more practical course. Who was going to go on living in Charne? There was no direct heir. During the lifetime of the present owner there never had been.

Nor, it seemed, had there been such an heir through several lifetimes before that. He remembered Grace Martineau as telling him—it had been in one of her mildly depressive states, which she seemed to have taught herself to mitigate through the making of confidences—that when she had married Charles and he had brought her to Charne she had scarcely expected to bear him a child. And, sure enough, she had never done so. Yet her expectation had rested only on a fanciful foundation. Already for three generations, it seemed, no child had been born in the house. Whether it had always been a Martineau who had been brought in to fill the gap, Appleby didn't know. A man sometimes has to change his name as well as his residence when he takes over such a place. Judith would have the facts. He must ask her.

He found that he had come to a halt, and was looking down into one of the two great stone basins round which this garden, now forsaken, had been organized. There was no reason at all why it should not brim with clear water, support the delicate cups of water lilies, afford adequate ooze and pasture for appropriately ornamental fish. Appleby suddenly saw that here was another gesture —unconsciously arrived at, it might be—by Martineau. A barren house. *Empty cisterns and exhausted wells.*

Bother the poets, Appleby told himself. He made to turn away, proposing to retrace his steps to the house— for no doubt he had been absent for as long as was civil. As he did so, he became aware that by the farther verge of the second basin—at noon, as it were, to his own six o'clock—stood the figure of Bobby Angrave. For a moment they looked at each other, oddly silent, across the two wide saucers of stone.

"Hullo!" Bobby then said. "What about getting a hose and filling them up? A nice surprise for Uncle Charles in the morning."

Chapter 3

"It would take the whole night," Appleby said prosaically. Walking over to Bobby Angrave, he added: "And your uncle might not be all that amused."

"It would take a lot to amuse Uncle Charles at present, poor devil." Bobby didn't stir from where he stood; he seemed fascinated by the great empty basin. "It's all pretty grim, wouldn't you say?"

"I don't suppose your aunt can hold on for long—or that one would wish her to."

"Can the old man? That seems to me the question."

"Your uncle?" Appleby was surprised. "He isn't ill too, is he?"

"Good Lord, no." Bobby had given an impatient shake of his head. It was an irritable—and irritating—mannerism of his when he judged people to be not as quick as they ought to be. "The old boy has twenty years to go. And that's just the point. How will he fill them, face them? They've been, you know, so fearfully close—Aunt Grace and he. The thing's driving him mad." Bobby broke off, picked up a tiny pebble, and dropped it into the

22

basin. "The parapet's curiously low, isn't it? An unnotice-able six inches. If it was full, in you could go in the dark and drown. As it is, you could break your neck."

"I hardly think so—though it mightn't be good for an arm or a leg." Appleby glanced at the young man curi-ously. "Of course, your aunt's illness is a tremendous strain on your uncle. But I don't think he'll go mad, or even in any way crack up. Somehow people don't—or not until afterwards."

"Perhaps so." Bobby picked up another pebble, made to throw it, thought better of this, and dropped it on the path. "But—do you know?—I can hardly stick it myself. That's why I made off just now, and took a turn in the wood. As for sitting down and writing a lot of damned Latin verses, the idea's absurd."

"I think you ought to try not to take it that way." Ap-pleby saw that Bobby Angrave was disturbed, and he obeyed an older man's impulse in such cases to hint some lesson of maturity. "There's always something to be said, Bobby, for just getting on with the job. Particularly if one can do it well, and if one likes it."

"I can do it well, all right." Bobby tossed this in con-temptuously. "But what sense is there in such tricks—here and now in the twentieth century? Absolutely none that I can see. That classical stuff is totally irrelevant. It simply turns its back on all the significant growing points of our time."

"I agree that there's an argument there." Appleby had refrained from smiling at Bobby's rather portentous vo-cabulary. "But why, in that case, are you turning yourself into a classical scholar?"

"Because I have a bloody great hole in my head, sir.

That's why. A hole where the sums should be."

"The sums?"

"The substantial mathematical ability without which no scientific mind can tick. That leaves, you see, Greek and Latin, along with the ridiculous parlour game they call philosophy, as the only royal road in the rat race."

"At least you're on that royal road?"

"Of course. My elegant Latinity, and what-not, will get me a fellowship—or into the Civil Service, absurdly enough, if I choose to go that way. But there's nothing more to it."

"I see." Bobby Angrave, it seemed to Appleby, possessed, after all, a fairly substantial power of absorbing himself in his own affairs.

"But that's not the point at the moment." It was almost as if Bobby had divined Appleby's thought. "Here's a woman going to die—quite naturally, and when she is on at least the fringes of old age. There ought to be nothing to it. Yet I feel a kind of animal terror when I think of it. Do you know what I mean?"

"I know what you mean by the animal terror."

"Does one go on experiencing it—after one has more or less had one's life? Or is it something only the young really feel, because death would cheat them of so much more?"

"They believe that death would cheat them of a great deal. But that may be an illusion."

"Yes, of course." Bobby gave his impatient headshake again. "But it doesn't answer my question."

"I think it's a matter of degree, in point both of frequency and intensity. But I've known very old people who were steadily and horribly afraid to die."

"We'd better go back to the house. This is getting morbid." Without waiting for a response, Bobby strode off towards the terrace. But within a dozen yards he had halted again, and waited for Appleby to catch up with him. "Do you believe in euthanasia?" he demanded.

"It's hardly a matter for belief or disbelief. It's obvious people ought to be got out of the world without intolerable suffering, whenever possible. And that may entail getting them out a little quicker than otherwise might be."

"There's clearly nothing in being dead." Bobby was moving forward again, but slowly. "All the old commonplaces are right there. We cease to be fortune's slaves, nay, cease to die, in dying. And so on."

"Yes," Appleby said.

"I suppose you've had a lot to do with death, sir? Violent death, I mean."

"I was up against a certain amount of it in the earlier part of my career." Appleby spoke a shade shortly. It must be something of quite recent occurrence, it struck him, that had excited this young man. He didn't see why he himself should be drawn by it into chatter about death. But Bobby Angrave went on. This time, he might have been trying to talk philosophy with his tutor.

"As to whether life is to be held desirable," he said, "the best opinions seem to differ. And, of course, mere death cannot be held either desirable or undesirable, since it is in fact not a state of being at all. Very well. Suppose that a killing disease—or suppose that a murderer—was coming at you. Would you have any rational ground for feeling resentment?" Bobby paused briefly. "But perhaps," he added, "that is not a meaningful question."

Appleby said nothing. This, he felt, was probably what Bobby's tutor would have done. They had come to a halt again at the foot of the steps leading up to the terrace. The house itself was invisible except for its topmost story. But there were several splashes of light which could come only from the music room. So everybody hadn't gone to bed.

"There's nothing in *being dead*," Bobby Angrave re-iterated. "Whether there's anything in *doing to death*, I don't know. It may well always be wicked. Certainly it can confer no positive benefit, but on the other hand it can annihilate despair and pain—which in practice comes to the same thing. So much for being dead and doing to death. Then there's *dying*. Certainly there is something to that: the kind of terror we were speaking about, and disagreeable physical sensations stretching from discomfort to agony. Of course some people are said to look forward to the hope of a joyful resurrection. But we can leave that out." Bobby paused again. He was in the enjoyment, Appleby supposed, of the persuasion that he was now handling his theme confidently and well, so that a clear alpha mark would be jotted down for him at the conclusion of the proceedings. "And so," he went on, "we come finally to *being died on*. And that really does give one pause."

"As your uncle is now being died on, you mean?"

"Just that, sir. It brings in the whole business of love."

"It certainly does."

"The cruel madness. May I fly that net."

Appleby was startled. For now the young man was really speaking out of some vivid experience—experience more sudden in its impact than could have been his gathered perception of the present state of affairs at Charne. And experience, surely, that was strictly traumatic, that might really wound or maim.

"I'm not clear," Appleby said slowly, "as to quite what this is about. But I think that the cruel madness may really be in what you are saying and feeling. For it's a denial of life to decline the richness of experience just because in the end there may be a bill to pay."

"People can do insane things, when in the net of love, passion, even affection. I know."

"For that matter, I know too. And I suppose one has simply to try to lend a hand."

"One has to extract some rational benefit from the mess."

"I can't see that we're talking about a mess."

"Well—say simply that one has to extract something out of the bizarre things people do. But I'm afraid I must be boring you frightfully, sir." Bobby produced this well-bred young man's conventional deference and diffidence with his familiar faint irony. It wasn't a quality for which there was much scope, Appleby supposed, in the fabricating of Latin verses. "In fact," Bobby went on, "we're rather a boring crowd at Charne."

"I've never been in the least of that opinion." Appleby said this firmly enough to constitute a rebuke. "And at least you've made your way here in quite a hurry, surely? The Oxford summer term can't be over."

"I cut out a week early. It's one of the advantages of being a prize boy. The old gentlemen indulge you. The subject of the composition I'm working on, you know, is *Rus in Urbe*. I told our president that I needed immediate *rus*, and that another week of *urbs* would be fatal to my starting at all. He beamed approval and pressed my hand at parting. And here I am."

"And everybody is pleased." Since Bobby was now laughing, Appleby laughed too. Like most young men, Bobby Angrave could strike his elders as tiresome enough at times. But one of the tiresome habits of youth is judging it necessary to lay a kind of smoke screen over their more generous impulses. It might well be that Bobby had cut short a thoroughly enjoyable term at Oxford in order to be with his uncle in this grim period. And he hadn't perhaps known that his aunt was clinging to her habit of filling—or quarter-filling—Charne with guests.

"What do you think of my cousin Martine Rivière?" Bobby asked abruptly.

"I haven't had much conversation with her, so far. She's clever, isn't she?"

"Yes—unlike that poor old thicky, Diana Page." Bobby began mounting the steps to the terrace. "I suppose Martine truddles Diana round as a kind of foil."

"I rather like Diana. As a matter of fact, you might find her—" Appleby checked himself. He had been about to say "a good deal more responsive in certain ways than Martine is ever likely to be." But if Bobby didn't know this—he told himself—it had perhaps better not be put in his head. For there was a lurking ruthlessness in Bobby —the ruthlessness, and perhaps even the chilly sensuality that goes with the theoretical mind. And Diana, after all, was very young. So, instead, he said lightly: "Is it Martine who has drawn you so quickly to Charne?"

"I had heard she was here."

"You find her attractive?"

"Oh, decidedly. In other circumstances, I can imagine

myself hunting her like mad. Of course, nothing much would come of it, even when everything had. But that might be the essence of the fun. Or that's my guess. But I'm totally ignorant, of course. The *mundus muliebris* isn't my affair. Still, I'm keeping an eye on Martine."

Appleby, beset by the peculiar discomfort that attends the reception of callow talk, said nothing. At least it would be an error to suppose that this accomplished young man didn't know his way around in the sphere just touched upon. There was no harm in that. Nevertheless he felt that, for the moment, he and Bobby Angrave had enjoyed enough of each other's company.

"I'll take one more turn along the terrace," he said, "and then follow you in. It will let me finish this cigar. I've always suspected that your aunt doesn't love the things."

"Aunt Grace is a fastidious woman." Bobby nodded, prepared to turn away. "It must make it all additionally formidable for her—wouldn't you say? I believe that dying doesn't merely have those terrors and agonies. It has its bad smells as well. Enjoy your cigar."

And Bobby walked off towards the house. The moonlight thrust a pale shadow before him on the gravel. Appleby stood still for a moment, and watched him go. He was far from convinced that Bobby had scored any sort of alpha during this curious half-hour.

Chapter 4

IT HAD BEEN to find Bobby Angrave, Appleby recalled, that he had separated himself from the party in the loggia and strolled out onto the grounds. Or rather he had made that an excuse for wandering away. And it suddenly came to him now, with an odd effect of belated discovery, that he had really been prompted to seek solitude by something quite different. Something—and he had wanted to find out what—had been twitching at his mind.

It was long professional habit that made him attentive to these obscure intimations of subliminal uneasiness. The detection of crime is a scientific process; he had watched it becoming progressively more so throughout his own professional career. But, like mathematics or modern physics, it is surprisingly dependent on intuitive factors, all the same. There are times at which the solution of a mystery can simply start up in the mind like a creation. Or it may lurk in the obscurer regions of the psyche and teasingly refuse to appear—or it may do no more than flash a fin, so to speak, above the surface of consciousness. It was second nature to Appleby to be sensitive to these tiny signals—so much so that he could not do other than attend to them when they came, even when it was in a context quite aside from his official life. Nowadays his crime-solving days were really over; he had to sit back and watch others at the job. But he still treated with unfailing respect these faint, momentary intimations that in this or that insignificant appearance lay something that ought to be attended to, that ought to be coaxed into revealing itself. The sense that there had been *something*, but that only deep down in his head did he know *what*, was still the keenest challenge that he knew. And he would attend to it in or out of season: it might be while reading a memorandum at his desk; it might be while taking tea with one of Judith's aunts. This was what had really brought him out of the loggia this evening. Here he was at Charne, miles away from any possibility of crime. But there had been *something*. Something that somebody had said had given that small familiar twitch to his mind, and he had left the party in the loggia—this itself by an almost unconscious process—in order to give it an opportunity less uncertainly to declare itself.

Well, it hadn't worked—perhaps because of the sudden manner in which Bobby Angrave had appeared on the scene. This was of no more importance than a failure to solve a chess problem or to find a clue in a crossword puzzle. Still, he didn't like being baffled. So now he gave his mind one last chance. Instead of simply walking down the terrace and back, he walked right round the house.

The door most frequently used for familiar comings and goings at Charne was in the west front. It lay in shadow at the moment, as did a diagonal slice of the broad paved yard separating it from a sprawl of stables and offices in part concealed behind a high stone wall. But as Appleby approached, a light went on, the door opened, and Friary could be seen and heard bidding good night to a briskly moving man who carried a small bag. This was Dr. Fell. He almost collided with Appleby as he made for his car, and then started back in an agitation that seemed to suggest either a sick or a very tired man. The two men exchanged greetings—perhaps with a slight awkwardness, since Appleby felt that he should scarcely inquire as to how the doctor had found his patient.

"It's wonderful how Friary gets back on the job," he said, by way of finding some casual remark.

"Back on the job?" Dr. Fell had a brusque manner. "I don't understand you."

"Oh, merely that he takes a little constitutional to the village every evening."

"Does he, indeed? It might be better if he didn't."

"You confirm my worst suspicions. At least, I suppose you do. Is Friary the local Lothario?"

"I wouldn't give it so romantic a name." Fell opened the door of his car, and shoved in his case. "Where did Martineau get hold of him, I wonder? It's usually a groom or an undergardener—or a footman, where they still happen—who makes a nuisance of himself when he has a strategic base in a house like this. At least you'd suppose the wretched girls might be safe from a butler."

"I see. Well, Friary might be described, I suppose, as a well-preserved butler. As to where Martineau picked him up, I haven't a notion. He may have a past, no doubt. But then we all do."

"Just what do you mean by that?"

Appleby was startled. The words had come, sharp and uncontrolled, from the obscurity of the car into which Dr. Fell had now climbed.

"I mean no more than I say," he said. "That's my habit."

"Sorry." Fell's voice was at once confused and apologetic. "I've had a damnable day—and you can guess I'm not happy about Mrs. Martineau. And now I must be off. Another couple of calls, as a matter of fact."

"I wouldn't like your job—although I wish I did as useful a one." Appleby stood back, waiting for Fell to slam his door. "Certainly not in winter. It's something you have to grow up to, I think."

"Well, I didn't. As you know. Good night."

At this the door did shut; the engine of the car came to life with an unimpressive rattle; Dr. Fell flicked on his lights, and drove off rapidly down the drive.

One can put a foot in it, Appleby thought. One can put *both* feet in it. But to put *each* foot in it successively is something of an achievement. And with Dr. Fell he seemed to have managed just that. To be so touchy, the man must have had some nasty check to his career, and a country doctor's job must irk him, even although he is good at it. Appleby turned back, and made his way round to the terrace. Perhaps Fell had thought he was hinting some knowledge of him, and proposing to dig out more. People did sometimes take it for granted that his profession must render him ceaselessly inquisitive about other folks' affairs. It was a misconception. And certainly he hadn't the slightest wish to learn more about Dr. Fell.

I do not love you, Dr. Fell . . . Nor hate you, nor care twopence for you either way. Appleby had come to

33

this conclusion on the matter—which showed that he was not very pleased with himself—when he rounded the corner of the house. Lights were still burning in the music room, but in addition to this somebody appeared to have returned to the loggia, for there was a light there also. Appleby strolled over to it, vaguely supposing it might be his wife. Judith too—although so inveterately sociable —was fond of occasional solitude.

It wasn't Judith; it was Diana Page. For a moment he thought she was asleep, for she was sitting hunched across a small table, with her head buried in her arms. Then he saw her shoulders heave, and heard the sound of convulsive sobbing. For some reason or other—and, like Dr. Gregory Fell's past, it was no business of his—Diana was having a good, a very good, cry. Appleby backed hastily, proposing to steal away. Only this time, unfortunately, he put his foot in it quite literally. Mrs. Martineau's gardening basket was on the ground by the loggia door. It contained, among other things, a small watering can. He stepped into the one, and overturned the other.

Diana jerked herself upright. She stared at Appleby, and Appleby stared at her. To step forward with some word, or some mere gesture of comfort might have seemed natural enough. But there are tears and tears— and Diana's, at the moment, somehow didn't prompt to consolation. She was, as Appleby had told himself earlier, little more than a child. It was a child's face that looked at him now. At the same time it was a face vividly sensuous—and with a sensuousness that had somehow been outraged or baffled. Angry mortification was what Appleby saw as he looked. It could be read as plainly as a book.

"Go away! You beastly, beastly spy, go away!" This came from Diana as a mere cry; she recited the words again and again; like a small girl in a tantrum, she waved her fists in front of her face.

It seemed undeniable to Appleby that he was having a bad evening. First Dr. Fell had put on a turn for him, and then—much more violently—this spoiled and sulky child. The judicious response to Diana, he supposed, would be stern words, briskly spoken. Or perhaps she ought to be slapped. Again, her hysteria might be controlled by means of the contents of the watering can. But on the whole it would probably be best to do exactly what she asked, and go away. Diana was in real misery, no doubt, but he was pretty sure its occasion didn't lie in any quarter where he could be helpful.

Having come to this conclusion, Appleby turned to leave the loggia. He found himself confronted by Friary.

"I beg your pardon, sir. I supposed there was nobody here, and came to turn off the light." As he said this, Friary was clearly enough taking in the scene before him. His expression might have been described as impassive —except, indeed, that this would have been to convey a wrong idea of him. It is the word conventionally applied to the features of upper servants when confronted with an untoward situation. But although Friary was undeniably an upper servant, there was something about him— Appleby reflected, not for the first time—that didn't quite go here with the character. It wasn't entirely a matter of his age. It wasn't even his physique—although that suggested itself as an athlete's—or anything definably out of the way in his manner. Perhaps it was something that ought to have been quite insignificant: how he held his hands, or the way he brushed his hair.

But what chiefly struck Appleby now was something quite different; it was a consciousness of the turn of speed Friary had put on between closing that distant door upon Dr. Fell and presenting himself here in the loggia. He must have had the shocking circumstance of a needlessly burning light very much on his mind. For a moment Appleby even had the strange thought that the man had been hastening to keep an assignation with Diana Page. If it were so, it wouldn't be quite right, this time, to tell himself that the matter was no business of his. Fortunately —or unfortunately—the idea was probably just another instance of his deplorable professional instinct to uncover intrigue. He simply wasn't fit—he sometimes told himself —to frequent normal society.

Meanwhile, Friary was still watching Diana—and doing so very much at his ease. Appleby saw no occasion for this.

"Thank you," he said briskly. "I'll see to the lights."

"Thank you, sir." Friary gave the ghost of a bow, and walked from the loggia. His manner of doing so wasn't remotely offensive. But even in this action there was something that left one wondering, all the same.

The interruption had at least served to pull Diana Page together. She had blown her nose; she was now dabbing at herself out of some small cosmetic contrivance.

"I was being silly," she said. "It's Mrs. Martineau. I can't bear it."

"Have you and Martine been staying at Charne long?" Appleby asked. He had better, he thought, say something that didn't controvert Diana's explanation of her conduct, although it wasn't an explanation he believed.

"A fortnight—nearly three weeks. It seems much longer."

"You mean it's rather dull?"

"Yes—no. I don't know. Martine and I ride together. And play golf. Tennis, when we can persuade Bobby and somebody else to join in."

"Is Bobby good?"

"Of course not. Bobby's a bit of a rabbit. But he's better than nobody."

As Diana said this, her glance strayed to the door through which Friary had just departed, with the result that Appleby had once more to clamp down on facile conjecture.

"Isn't there much in the way of a neighbourhood, as they used to say? Young people for tennis, and so forth, not too far off?"

"There must be lots of people in the town, but the Martineaus don't seem to have much to do with them. At Weston Place—that's the nearest house like this—there's only a crowd of frumpy girls." Diana said this with a considerable effect of grievance. "At Feathers there's just the one daughter, Simona, who's frightfully stylish and deb, and does her best to monopolize any young men there are. Ronny Clandon at Proby used to be a resource. I liked Ronny. But, of course, he was binned."

"Binned? You mean the poor young man went mad?"

"Oh, no. Ronny just took an awful lot of drugs, and his parents got in a panic. They're terribly square." Diana looked at Appleby appraisingly. "That means something like old-fashioned," she added.

"Yes—I think I've heard the term."

"The funny thing about drugs is that they seem to be

37

catching."

"Well, yes. I've heard that too."

"The same thing happened to Tim Gorham."

"And did they bin him?"

"Oh, much worse. Tim was sent to Australia."

"I'm very sorry to hear it. Did Tim live near here too?"

"Oh, yes. He was a friend of Ronny's. They were both frightfully rich, although hardly more than twenty-one. Tim had an Aston Martin DB5, and its windows worked by electricity. So it was a great shame."

"An absolute calamity," Appleby agreed gravely. "But shall we go back to the music room? It's where evenings here usually end."

"Very well." Diana gave a final touch to her nose, and stood up. "Sometimes," she said, "I think they never will end."

Chapter 5

THE MUSIC ROOM was the largest apartment at Charne—large enough to make one keep wondering how it fitted so unobtrusively into a house the total dimensions of which appeared, from the outside, as of no more than the moderate order. It would have appeared larger still if it hadn't been cluttered with too much furniture—the Martineaus, like many prosperous people, having been for a good many generations inclined to acquire costly and handsome objects without an answering willingness to part with existing possessions no whit inferior in these regards. If this made it a shade oppressive, so too did its principal decorative feature: an almost unbroken band of large paintings by Holman Hunt, executed upon canvas but applied to the walls within a panelling rather heavily embellished in gold. The series was understood to represent *Shakespeare's Use of Song*. There was Orsino, calling for more of the Food of Love. There was Desdemona, delivering herself of "Sing willow, willow, willow." There was the unfortunate Christopher Sly, being assured that Apollo was playing for him. There was Jessica, never merry when she heard sweet music. There was a great deal more—and the cumulative effect, although no doubt apposite in a music room, was undeniably on the noisy side. The Pre-Raphaelites were, on the whole, lucky with their colourmen; their pigments don't fade or tone down; these exercises of Holman Hunt's were as pristine in their crammed detail as they had ever been. They rather commanded one, therefore, as often as one entered the room.

They rather commanded Appleby now, as he came in with Diana Page in front of him. Indeed, he found himself actually pausing as if to consult them—or to respond, it might be, to some tiny signal which one of these scenes or characters had contrived to flash at him. In a moment the sensation was gone again. He remembered that he had experienced something very similar only a short time before.

Of the house party as it had assembled in the loggia, only Mrs. Martineau was no longer in evidence. Her husband, erect and spare, stood in front of the fireplace; above his head Lear's Fool, a wisp of motley on the darkening heath, regaled his master and the faithful Kent on the theme: *He that has a little tiny wit*. Bobby Angrave was certainly right in saying that his uncle had another twenty years in him. Many men similarly circumstanced, it occurred to Appleby, if looking forward to such a span of time, would judge it proper that a place like Charne should not be without a mistress. It was hard to imagine Charles Martineau married again. And it was harder, somehow, to imagine Charne without Grace, who had simply come to it as a bride, than without Charles, who had inherited it. But women sometimes do grow into a house in that way, and take on the main burden of guarding and expressing its continuity. It would be Mrs. Martineau who would be chiefly horrified if, say, it were suggested that the Holman Hunts be detached from the walls for despatch to a museum, or even that a little more room be made here for simple moving about.

How much Mrs. Martineau did stand for Charne was emphasized at the moment by the mere fact that, since she had gone to bed, Martine Rivière was in some slight manner acting as hostess during these last social exchanges of the evening. Martine was a very different sort of person from her aunt. As Mrs. Martineau's niece, it seemed unlikely that she would ever inherit the property, although Appleby rather understood that Charne was in no way tied up or entailed. But suppose she married her cousin Bobby Angrave, who did seem a likely heir—what would happen then? In the fulness of time poor Holman Hunt would certainly vanish in favour of whatever might be held in vogue in that particular future; the place would be given a new and contemporary note; there would be a good deal of entertaining of the sort that reflects less a play of personal sympathies and attractions than a policy or line in some chosen field of manoeuvre—political, literary, artistic, or whatever. No harm in that. And whether, in these circumstances, Charne would continue to be a barren house was an open question. Appleby found he couldn't imagine Martine Rivière's children by Bobby Angrave. But this didn't mean that they mightn't, one day, be swarming all over the place. Dimly, one rather saw them as little eggheads—and chilly ones at that. But at least Charne would give them a chance. They could first paddle and then swim in those great stone ba-

41

sins; they could be Cherokees or Martians in Charne Wood.

Meanwhile, Charne was rather massively as it had been for a long time. The "improvements" about which the young husband and wife had talked in the little belvedere long ago must themselves have been of a conservative order. It was true that the house now preserved an even temperature, summer and winter, throughout; true that water, hot and cold, ran into its every corner; true that it displayed that proliferation of elegant ivory telephones convenient in an age in which it is politic to converse with servants rather than baldly summon them. But these were superficial changes. Essentially, two wars, each with its succeeding peace, had left Charne very much as it had been.

Abandoning Diana—which seemed the tactful thing to do—Appleby moved over to Martine. She was very far from being a charmless person. Indeed, Nature had formed her perfect—as a statue may be perfect, for she had a figure from which one could almost imagine the most lusty bachelor as stripping the garments with an aesthetic rather than an erotic intent. On the other hand, she didn't suggest herself as a creature without passion; it was simply that she rather left one wondering under just what circumstances this marble Galatea would spring to life.

"My aunt has made her excuses," Martine said, a shade formally. "She has gone to bed. How much she likes to have her friends around her! But it tires her, all the same." She pointed to a table. "Won't you get yourself some whisky, Sir John? Friary is locking up."

"Thank you. Is Friary keen on security? It's a quality

commending itself to a policeman."

"I think he is. And quite a lot could be carried off by enterprising burglars, wouldn't you say?"

"Well, yes. One hardly sees them getting away with the Holman Hunts."

"No. But the spoils of Charne are very considerable, all the same."

"I'm sure they are. The burglars could fill several sacks with Georgian silver alone." Appleby hoped he wasn't looking at Martine Rivière too curiously. He had a notion that burglars were not very much in her head. "If they succeed," he went on, "I believe your aunt would be more upset than your uncle."

"In a way, yes. Aunt Grace doesn't greatly prize material things in themselves. But she would certainly see the Martineau silver—although much of it is quite ugly—as part of an order it would be very dreadful to see violated."

"Do you sympathize with that—I mean in a general way? I think of you, Martine, as rather *avant-garde*, and not terribly impressed with the virtue of walking in the ancient ways, just for their own sake. Is that wrong?"

"In the light of one's own needs, one should make a rational use of what comes to one."

"I suppose so. Yes, I suppose I've always tried to do that myself." Appleby studied the small splash of whisky in his glass. Again he didn't want to stare at this young woman as if she were an enigma. Just this sentiment, it had occurred to him, might have been expressed by her cousin Bobby. In fact he recalled that "rational" was one of Bobby's pet words. "I imagine," he said casually, "that you and Bobby have seen a good deal of each other since childhood. Do you find that you have much in common?"

"There are things that we are both interested in. I wouldn't call us natural allies. I don't think we've ever been much prompted to form a common front. Uncle Charles, you know, wants us to get married. Do you think it would be a good idea?"

"I think it would be very rash to give an opinion." Appleby, who thought of himself as an elderly person of conventional mind, had been a little surprised by this bald question. "No doubt," he added demurely, "you will yourself give the matter thought."

"Oh, but I have. And Bobby too, of course. It does represent one possible solution."

"Ah, yes." Appleby wasn't very clear what this was about—or why this normally reticent girl should be entering upon the subject merely, it seemed, for the sake of making conversation. Her tone hardly suggested that what a "solution" had to be found for was any very passionate involvement of human hearts. Presumably what was in question was the disposition of property—and, in particular, Charne itself. Appleby had been thinking about this only a few minutes before. But he saw no reason to enter further into the topic now, and his next words were intended to dismiss it lightly. "Well, you both have a little time to think about it. It isn't as if the years were beginning to pass very noticeably over either of you."

"I'm two years older than Bobby. Don't you think it shows?"

"Looking at both of you, I shouldn't have an idea, either way." Appleby reflected that this was quite true, as far as any guessing at birthdays went. On the other hand,

Martine struck him as more mature than her cousin, by a long way. It is often so, when one sets a twenty-year-old young woman beside a male contemporary almost straight from an English public school. Bobby Angrave, of course, carried around a lot of precocious intellectual sophistication. But this only served to make the point more evident.

"Then I must be very well preserved," Martine said. "So is Uncle Charles, wouldn't you say?"

"Yes, indeed. Everybody says that."

"Aunt Grace is against it."

"Against your Uncle Charles's being—?" Appleby was astray before this inconsequence.

"No, no." Martine shook her head with an impatience very like Bobby's. "Aunt Grace is against the idea of the marriage. She would like me to do better."

"You mean that she would like you to marry a millionaire or a nobleman?" Appleby was coming not at all to care for this conversation.

"Not necessarily. But she thinks Bobby is no good."

Appleby put down his glass, and looked round for his wife. But Judith was at the other end of the room with Diana Page, with whom she seemed to be in rather more than casual talk. And Charles Martineau had moved into a window embrasure with Bobby. The two men were studying some map or plan laid out on a large table there. The picture, Appleby suddenly saw, was very much that of a landed proprietor, anxious to do nothing on his estate without canvassing the interest and approval of his heir. It did seem as if the Martineaus, in most things so profoundly at one, differed in this one area of their concern.

"In that particular relation," Martine said.

"I beg your pardon?" Appleby supposed that his attention must have strayed.

"I don't mean that Aunt Grace supposes Bobby to be a frightful cad or anything." Martine appeared to perceive that her conversation had been unamiable. "She just doesn't see him at Charne. And I don't think she sees *me* at Charne—although, of course, it is only the marriage that could make that a possibility. Even, you see, although she is much fonder of me than I deserve."

Appleby again found himself wondering why all this was being thrown at him. There was nothing impulsive about Martine. But he ranked, he supposed, as an old friend of the family—and with the family, too, Judith had that tenuous actual relationship. So perhaps the proposal was to enlist the Applebys' support for some plot which Martine was hatching. Appleby was far from thinking this a good idea. He was about to find some form of words to make this clear when Martine went off at another tangent.

"Do you know Barbara Gillingham?" she asked.

"No. I don't think I've heard of her."

"She's coming tomorrow. Aunt Grace has asked her. She's a sprightly widow."

"Really?" Appleby looked at his watch, not much concerned that this wasn't wholly polite. "By Jove! It's getting quite late."

"Aren't you interested in Mrs. Gillingham?"

"Well, no—or not greatly, just at the moment. I've no doubt she's a charming woman, whom it will be a pleasure to meet."

"How stuffy of you, Sir John! Or is it, rather, just how

discreet? You don't even want to know her age?"

"My dear Martine, I've no objection to being *told* her age. Indeed, I'll *ask* you, if you like. How old is this Mrs. Gillingham?"

"I don't really know." It seemed to amuse Martine to give this answer. "Perhaps she's what they call of uncertain age. Or perhaps she's precisely *not* that. She's definitely not beyond childbearing." Martine Riviére paused on this. She was looking serious again. "And that is why she interests my aunt."

"It certainly isn't why she interests your uncle—if she does interest him."

"Not at present, Sir John. But my Aunt Grace is a far-sighted woman."

Chapter 6

"THE PENDLETONS are coming for the weekend," Judith Appleby said. She and her husband were walking on the terrace after breakfast next morning.

"The young ones—or Edward and Irene?"

"Edward and Irene."

"Oh, dear! Well, that won't be much more fun for the bored young people on the spot. They don't seem too pleased with each other, would you say? Incidentally, Mrs. Gillingham is coming too."

"Who on earth is Mrs. Gillingham?"

"I thought you might know. If she's who, or what, Martine says she is, then I can tell you *why* the Pendletons are coming. And, for that matter, why we've come. When Grace, I mean, is so very ill." Appleby glanced up at the house. "Let's go a bit farther afield," he said. "Into the wood."

"Yes, let's do that." Judith walked for some paces in silence. "You think it's odd having guests at all?"

"Not really—although some people wouldn't. But it would be odd to have only Mrs. Gillingham. Hence our larger gathering."

"Whatever has Martine been telling you?"

"Chiefly that this Mrs. Gillingham—Barbara Gillingham—is a sprightly widow, well able to bear children."

"Let's take this path." Judith pointed. "It goes up by the stream to the belvedere. But I can't believe it—what you seem to mean, or make Martine mean."

"It may well be just a bad guess. But she was quite explicit."

"It was some kind of hard, tasteless joke. What they call a sick joke."

"Give the poor child a little credit. It wasn't that."

"Besides, I've rather supposed that Charles would be happy if Bobby and Martine were to—"

"Quite so. And Bobby and Martine know it. They're even considering it, in a bloodless kind of way—or so I seemed to gather."

"Surely Grace should approve of *that*? It would provide for Martine, who is her sister's child, as well as for Bobby, who is the child of Charles's sister."

"Yes, but I think the point is—or one point is—that they are both a little far out. Not born for Charne, and not really quite fitted for it."

"How deep this pool is!"

They had now climbed about halfway to the crown of the wood, and were pausing by the largest of the pools through which the little stream passed. It was reed-fringed, and showed as dark brown except for a few bars of gold where the morning sun caught it. At its farther side a broad archipelago of water lilies were opening. Everything around was quite still.

"Is it deep? I don't see how you can tell."

"I've a quite intimate knowledge of it." Judith walked to the verge, laughing. "Yes—it was just here. I tried to ride my pony through it. There was an awful row. I wonder what the little fish are? It seems nonsense to me."

"What seems nonsense?"

"That Bobby and Martine should be excluded because not precisely right." Judith turned away from the pool, and walked on. "They might make do—and that's the wise and human thing to be content with."

"I rather agree. But Grace is a very sick woman, and the judgment of sick people is sometimes not like ours. I suspect the real point to be that she has borne Charles no children. It imposes some burden of irrational guilt upon her. So she wants to go, before it's not too late. But on her own terms. The sponge is to be passed over the slate—"

"Did Martine say all this?"

"No, but I've no doubt she understands it well enough. The second Mrs. Martineau, formerly Mrs. Gillingham, is to bring Charne an heir. And Charles may well live to see his son into his majority."

"But, John, surely that would be to cheat Martine a little—and to cheat Bobby a great deal? Charles would never do it."

"His wife's wish—Grace's wish—might be sacred to him. I believe that's the phrase."

"I think it's morbid rubbish. And I can't imagine that Charles himself has an inkling of the plan—if it really *is* a plan."

"Perhaps not. Perhaps it is going to be communicated to him this evening or the next, in one of those revived chats between the Martineaus in this belvedere we're

50

climbing to. Then, of course, there is Mrs. Gillingham. We don't know whether *she* knows. She may yet have to be squared too—if that's the word."

"It's decidedly not the word. And, on consideration, I think there's a certain nobility in Grace's feeling the way you are suggesting she does."

"I don't agree." Appleby was suddenly obstinate. "If you and I had no children, and I found you making such a plan, I'd be very angry with you."

"We don't own Charne."

"If we did, I'd like it even less. I can understand setting a more or less mystical value on perpetuation through progeny—although I hope I'd be sensible enough to see that the world is never likely to go short of young men and women hard at work feeding the sacred flame. But Charne isn't a sacred flame. It's just a great big house, and a dozen farms in process of disappearing beneath a rash of little dog-kennelly villas, and a great deal of money, no doubt, in stocks and shares. I see no virtue whatever in a particular accumulation of material wealth going to a son rather than to a nephew, or for that matter to a nephew rather than to a cat-and-dog home."

"John, how very strongly your early radicalism is bubbling up in you again. You're little better than a Bolshevik. They ought never to have given you that K."

"I took it only to have a Ladyship about the house."

"Here's the belvedere. Let's take a look inside."

The small building before which they now stood was circular in shape. It might have been described as an elongated stone drum, surrounded by Ionic pillars and crowned with a low dome.

"I suppose it's elegant," Appleby said. "But I don't see much sense in it. Why call a thing a belvedere when it's impossible to see anything from inside? There's not a window in the whole building."

"There's the big door. You can keep that open, and it faces down the main vista. Or you can sit between the pillars, and look out any way you please."

"I seem to remember it isn't dark inside, although it ought to be. But I don't recall why."

"There's a circular hole in the roof. Like the Pantheon. I think it's called an eye."

"And the sky peers through the eye. I, God, see you. Yes, the belvedere is certainly elegant. But it seems to me to be designed to look *at* rather than to look *from*. The Italian word is ambiguous, come to think of it. The Germans are much more definite. They'd call such a place an *Aussichtspunkt*. No ambiguity about that."

They had now mounted the three or four steps leading to the door of the building, and they turned for a moment to glance at the view. A small outcrop of rock had been used to perch the belvedere on, so that one looked directly out into a middle distance. Round the base of the rock ran a narrow path, protected here by a rustic handrail from a farther miniature precipice beyond which the trees thickened again.

"That's where the clock goes by," Judith said, pointing to the path.

"The clock?"

"Friary. Don't you remember? On his punctual return from the village. The Martineaus sit up here, and Friary goes by, quite unaware of them, more or less at their feet."

"It doesn't really seem to me much of a place to come and sit in of an evening. Chilly, for one thing."

"Open the door. You'll find it quite snug, in spite of the eye in the roof. Electricity laid on, and one or two thoroughly comfortable chairs."

"The door won't open." Appleby had tried the handle, and was now turning away. "Charles must keep it locked."

"How very odd! It never used to be like that. It's probably only stuck. Give it a good shove."

Vigorously, if not particularly pertinaciously, Appleby did as he was told. His efforts produced only a hollow reverberation from within.

"No good," he said. "Shall we walk downhill again?"

"I think we might climb to the very top first. Or at least to where the stream starts. There's one of the grottoes just there. It's odd that a stream should emerge almost at the summit of a hill."

They continued to move at leisure through the wood. There was no wind, and one would have been inclined to say that the only sound was the murmur of the stream and the growing hum of insects beginning to respond to the warmth of the day. But, behind this, it was possible to hear the intermittent noise of traffic which spoke of the encroaching town.

"Has Charles sold any land?" Appleby asked.

"I don't think so. He'd be very unlikely to do anything of the sort, of his own free will. As the city spreads, I suppose he might find himself up against some power of compulsory purchase one day."

"Bobby might sell—if he inherited the place."

"I don't see why. There's a lot more than the house

53

and the estate. He wouldn't be likely to need money."

"He might do it by way of being what he calls rational."

"If Grace saw the possibility of that, it certainly wouldn't put Bobby in her good books."

"He's not there as it is. Hullo!" Appleby had come to a halt. "Here's the first grotto—the Chinese one, isn't it?"

"Yes. It's by the elder Halfpenny."

"Halfpenny?" Appleby looked at his wife suspiciously. "He sounds most implausible."

"He's entirely authentic. William Halfpenny—and he had a son called John. He published *Rural Architecture in the Chinese Taste,* bang in the middle of the eighteenth century."

"Well, at least a grotto in the Chinese taste is an absurdity. The Chinese don't have grottoes. How could they? China consists exclusively of large rivers, wandering through rice fields and mud flats."

"But they have a Great Wall—so there must be plenty of stone somewhere."

As they conducted this absurd conversation, Appleby and Judith had come to a halt in front of the grotto. It had been created partly by excavation and partly out of stone heaped up in artful disorder and carved to simulate water-worn rock. A couple of rather sheepish dragons guarded the entrance; their tails rose to support a sculptured trophy, vaguely oriental in suggestion, of conglomerated helmets, spears and shields; a cold breath blew out of the place, and there was a sound of rapidly dripping water.

"It was designed that there should be a cascade inside," Judith said. "But Halfpenny never got round to the machinery. The whole affair was to have been quite elaborate. You can see how the walls are plastered with rock crystal and shells and what used to be called fossil bodies. But, although they dug some way into the hill, it never came to very much."

"Delusions of grandeur," Appleby said. "Let's move on."

"But look!" Judith was pointing upwards. "Violets—right at the top. It's late for them to be in flower still. I'd like to take some down to Grace. Do you think we could gather a bunch?"

"I suppose I could scramble." Appleby was regarding the sides of the grotto rather doubtfully. "It's all made to look more precarious than it is."

"Of course it is. All these chunks of oddly perched rock have been there for a couple of centuries. They must be bedded in cement, or something. We'll both climb."

They climbed—for the violets had niched themselves almost at the apex of the roughly formed arch which constituted the entrance to the grotto. Appleby gave Judith a final hand to the top, and watched her as she gathered a small bunch of the flowers. Then he looked round about him.

"There's a bit of a view from up here," he said. "You can see the belvedere again."

"So you can. And there's a glimpse of the roof of the house. But look!"

From where they stood they could just see, at an oblique angle, one leaf of the broad door of the belvedere. It had opened as Judith spoke, and the figure of a man had come out of the building. He stood for a moment, seeming to look carefully—even rather warily—about him. He turned round, and they could see that it was Charles Martineau. He closed the door gently, and appeared to lock it. Then he took another glance around him, slipped something into his pocket, and walked quickly away.

"But how strange!" Judith said. "Charles must have been in the belvedere when we tried the door a few minutes ago. I don't see how he can have failed to hear us."

"He lets his own people wander about the wood. And the villagers too, I expect. They're his tenants, I suppose. He probably thought we were inquisitive children making a nuisance of themselves."

"We must ask him."

"Must we?" Appleby was frowning. "Perhaps we oughtn't to be spying around."

"What an extraordinary idea!" But Judith was frowning too. "You're not hunting after a mystery, are you?"

"Of course not. But Charles had shut himself in. If he wasn't asleep, which seems improbable, he must have heard and recognized our voices. So my notion of his taking us for children or strangers won't do. He simply didn't want to be disturbed. And he might rather the thing weren't referred to."

"But it's awkward. He heard us, and now we've seen him. Just to keep mum—"

"Well, yes. But remember that he and Grace occasionally come up here of a summer evening—and in rather a nostalgic way. Charles sometimes comes up by himself and thinks about things. Put it like that. He heard us and didn't want to be bothered with us. If we'd thought, we might have concluded it rather oafish to go near the place at all, just at present. So we'll simply keep quiet."

"You're perfectly right." Judith had arranged her violets, and was preparing to begin the scramble down from the top of the grotto. "But didn't you think there was—?"

"Yes. Charles came out of the place in a fashion I can't quite account for. But it's not my business to try." Appleby laughed as he led the way down to the path. "It's something I seem to be telling myself regularly, just at present."

"I think I hear a car on the drive. We can at least speculate about that. Perhaps Bobby Angrave has got back. He drove off to town in a great hurry immediately after breakfast. I asked him why he was doing without a second cup of coffee, and he said he had an immediate duty to visit the good poor. Bobby has rather a freakish sense of humour."

"Yes. But the car is just as likely to belong to my touchy friend, Dr. Fell. I'm afraid he has to turn up pretty frequently now. Or it may be the enigmatical Mrs. Gillingham."

"Let's go down and see," Judith said. "And we can do as much guessing about her as we please."

Chapter 7

IT WAS CERTAINLY not Dr. Fell's car. It might be Mrs.
Gillingham's, if the sprightly character of that lady's
widowhood included driving around in a very grand
limousine indeed. The Aston Martin DB5 formerly
owned by that hapless expatriate Tim Gorham, Appleby
reflected, could be shoved into the inside of this monster
without anybody noticing it. And this extravagant calcu-
lation reminded him of something.

"By the way," he said, as he and Judith moved towards the house, "did I see you trying to get some sense
out of Diana Page just before we went to bed last
night?"

"Almost that. I did have a slight impulse to busy-
body."

"So had I, just a littler earlier. Have you a feeling she
has done something foolish?"

"Well, either that she has done, or that she may be
about to."

"I thought her quite lively at first." Appleby broke off.
"That car, by the way, is the Pendletons'. I've just recog-

nized it."

"Of course. Top surgeons have to parade such things. What an odd hour to turn up." Judith stopped in her tracks. "John—Edward Pendleton wouldn't be here professionally?"

"It hadn't occurred to me, but I suppose he might. Or semi-professionally. One makes desperate, groping gestures in Charles's position. He may have told Fell he'd just like his very old friend Edward Pendleton around. But I imagine that surgery is a thing of the past with Grace."

"Yes," Judith said, and for a few moments they walked in silence. "Why did you think Diana lively?" she asked.

"Well, she sometimes teases Bobby Angrave quite effectively, if in rather a childish way. Bobby says she's thick, and I suppose he's right."

"Dangerously thick, almost. She would be terribly easy to take in."

"Do you know anything about her people? Are they wealthy?"

"I've hardly heard anything about them. Diana tags around with Martine, and nobody else seems much to bother about her." Judith considered for a moment. "I had a notion last night that, if we hadn't just been in a corner of the music room before bedtime, and with people drifting around, Diana might have come out with something. My guess about her is a broken home, divorces, wardships, trustees and so on—all against a background of considerable affluence."

"Her conversation suggests assumptions that go with that, poor child. By the way, Fell's car is down there too. He's tucked it away rather discreetly, but I can just see it in a corner of the stable yard. Let's go round that way. We may meet him coming out."

"You want to meet him?"

"Well, yes. I was inept with him, you know, last night. He looked oddly under the weather, and I said something stupid about what it takes to be a G.P. So I'd like to be civil now."

"Very well." Judith sounded resigned. "But what you really mean is that the man has stirred your curiosity."

"Perhaps so," Appleby said.

Sure enough, Dr. Fell emerged from the west door just as he had done the evening before. Daylight was doing nothing to improve his appearance. There was something haggard about him, and almost hunted. Nor did he seem conversable, for although he now stopped to talk, it was with a detectable air of doing so only because the Applebys were planted squarely in his path.

"Good morning," Appleby said. "I don't know that you have met my wife? Judith, this is Dr. Fell."

Dr. Fell responded to this introduction correctly but without enthusiasm, so that there was an awkward moment in which conversation failed to happen.

"Do you know," Judith said, "that there are still violets in Charne Wood? We found a great clump on the top of the Chinese grotto, and I have brought these for Mrs. Martineau."

"But she still walks there from time to time, doesn't she?" It was not very felicitously that Dr. Fell produced this; he might have been suggesting that Judith's proposal was a tactless one.

"She would hardly scramble to the top of the grotto."

"Of course not." Dr. Fell now seemed to be producing an equally clumsy retraction. "It's remarkable that she gets around at all." For a moment he studied the bunch of flowers in Judith's hand with gravity. They might have been something under a microscope that spoke sharply of mortality. "I know that you are old friends of the family," he said suddenly. "I suppose you realize that these are the last violets my patient is likely to see."

"Yes, I think we realize that."

"They are very lovely." Unexpectedly, Dr. Fell put out a hand in what—although it revealed a gross tremor —was an oddly sensitive gesture. He touched one of the leaves in which the violets were cradled. "Somebody speaks of them as 'uttering the earth in magical expression.' But I suppose it is what we all do, flesh and grass alike, for a time."

This—being what the eighteenth century would have called a Serious Thought—produced a moment's silence. Fell had spoken quite unaffectedly. He wasn't, Appleby found himself thinking, at all a commonplace person.

"Will you allow me to say something that may sound uncivil?" Fell turned from Judith to Appleby to say this. "The sooner you all go away, the less unhappy I shall be."

Whether this was uncivil or not, it was notably inoffensive. Although he had his curiously awkward moments, Dr. Fell decidedly understood the conversation of gentlemen. At least, Appleby thought, that was how Judith's uncles—inveterately old-world characters—would have expressed the point. A less antique judgment might say simply that there was nothing provincial about Dr. Fell. He carried around with him a certain ease and authority which seemed to come from a larger world.

"What you say doesn't surprise me," Appleby said. "My wife and I have talked about the thing. But we are all here, you know, by Grace's wish. It's something that —more than ever at the moment—she has a right to."

"The point isn't at all likely to escape me." Fell was impatient. "But there are limits, it seems to me. Mrs. Martineau tells me that later today there will be turning up some woman who has scarcely ever been to Charne before. And only half an hour ago there were arrivals in an affair like a battleship. Martineau should have more sense. The strain on his wife is quite untimely."

"And here," Judith said, "the crew of the battleship come. Like a boarding party, one might say."

This was true. Round the corner of the house came the new arrivals. They were unaccompanied by their host. The Pendletons, it was to be conjectured, having arrived at Charne at a somewhat early hour, had murmured their wish to wander round without fuss. And here they were.

It was believed by the dramatist Strindberg that professional cooks are invariably persons sanguine, fleshy and bloated through a mysterious battening upon the life-blood of those whom they are employed to nourish. A similar mechanism is sometimes asserted to operate in the case of surgeons. But Edward Pendleton was far from bearing this out. From his exquisite silver-grey hair to his wholly appropriate weekend-in-the-country brown shoes he was eminently the man who has kept his form through all the severities of an arduous calling. His figure was that of a young athlete—and a fencer's, one told oneself, rather than a footballer's. And to this his wife Irene very adequately matched up. If she a little too clearly suggested what her own portrait would be like when encountered on the walls of the Royal Academy—for she seemed very much a product of delicately applied glazes —she was yet so nice a specimen of her particular world that one would have felt wholly churlish in thinking to scratch a lacquer so elaborately contrived for one's delectation. The Pendletons were cordial and perhaps even kindly people; they possessed and exercised every art for putting you at your ease; it wasn't at all their fault—you had guiltily to feel—if the total effect they projected fell a little short of the wholly sympathetic.

The Pendletons approached the Applebys with appropriate expressions of pleasurable expectation now gratified. The Applebys, bracing themselves, responded with actual gestures of a decorous joy. Dr. Fell stayed quite still—but as these ritual approaches did not concern him, there was nothing out of the way in that. Dr. Fell, however, had to be introduced, since it would hardly have been proper to let a professional colleague of the eminent Edward Pendleton simply fade into the background. Appleby was about to perform this office when he became aware that the two men were already known to each other.

It wasn't that they had broken into speech, or given each other so much as a nod. Dr. Fell remained immobile, looking at Pendleton. His posture held the rigidity to which there is conventionally applied the rather violent term "transfixed." Pendleton, although his own relaxed stance didn't change, was looking straight at Fell with an expression of dispassionate scrutiny which didn't suggest itself as a stranger's. And then Appleby had said something, and Pendleton was stepping forward with an extended hand.

"How do you do," he said, with brisk cordiality. He had, if ever so faintly, the air of a man making a gesture. "May I introduce you to my wife? Irene, this is Dr.—" Pendleton paused in the kind of polite apology of a man who has failed to pick up an unfamiliar name.

"Fell," Fell said.

"I am so sorry. Dr. Fell."

Mrs. Pendleton broke into gracious speech. She had, one felt, scores of obscure medical practitioners presented to her every week. Fell listened with a near approach to silence. When Mrs. Pendleton eventually made a flicker of a pause, he bowed and walked away.

"What an interesting man!" Mrs. Pendleton said. She didn't look pleased. Interesting men, one was constrained to feel, represented a category she judged it unnecessary to approve of. "Judith, dear, how delightful you should be at Charne! We must have a tremendous gossip." The emphasis with which she said this failed, somehow, to suggest that there was much substance in the proposition. But she took Judith by the arm, and walked her away.

"How splendid the place looks!" Edward Pendleton said to Appleby. "I always enjoy coming to rusticate at Charne."

"It's ceasing to be all that rustic. The town will be lapping round it in no time."

"I know, I know! Terrible, isn't it? It was Hitler's war that did it, wouldn't you say? Producing, I mean, as a kind of undesigned by-product, the first true dawn of scientific medicine. And that—my own trade, and all those wretched moulds and antibiotics—ensuring the survival and proliferation of millions of totally unnecessary little people. Sad, sad!"

Edward Pendleton, in fact, had his own kind of chat. Appleby listened to it for some time, and then asked a question.

"That chap Fell," he said. "I rather got the impression you'd met him before?"

"Fell?" Pendleton looked blank.

"The Martineaus' G.P.—whom we met a minute ago."

"Ah, yes. I'm not aware of ever having spoken to him. What a splendid oak that is, straight ahead! I envy Charles his timber. It's something one can't summon round oneself in a hurry. Now, tell me about the family, my dear fellow."

Appleby told Edward Pendleton about the family. But he wondered why he had been so firmly shut up.

Chapter 8

GRACE MARTINEAU now no longer appeared at lunchtime, but when she was well enough she liked one or another member of the household to join her for this meal in her room. On the present occasion this distinction fell to Mrs. Gillingham, who had arrived just after noon. It was impossible not to be impressed by Mrs. Gillingham, or even to impugn her entire suitability for the difficult role which her hostess was conjectured as being minded to assign her. She had driven herself up in a car which, although less splendid than the Pendleton battleship, seemed to speak of rather more than modest competence. It was not to be conjectured, therefore, that she had an eye on Charne—if, so far, she could be said to have an eye on it at all—out of any pressing sense of material necessity. Again Mrs. Gillingham had, it appeared, a daughter, and this child could be viewed as offering reassurance in two ways. She was conveniently tucked away in a suitably expensive boarding school, and the circumstance of her existing at all proved her mother to have passed an apprenticeship in the crucial power of bearing

66

children.

Perhaps these facts in themselves would not have taken Barbara Gillingham very far in any mature regard. But there had to be added to them the evident circumstance of her being a very nice woman. Moreover, her good looks—for she had good looks—suggested themselves as of a kind that would continue into an autumnal phase, and her cultivation—which one similarly couldn't doubt —seemed of a kind less showy than hard-wearing. But, above all, Mrs. Gillingham incontestably had the gift of repose. She wasn't stodgy; it would have been misleading and unfair even to describe her as placid; and if she was equally remote from being sprightly—which had been Martine's derogatory word—there was no reason to apprehend that she would be without her moments of exhilarating vivacity. All in all, she was formidable. Martine's eyes might be said to have narrowed on her—and Bobby Angrave's, correspondingly, to have rounded— the moment she entered the house.

Nor—and this was unusual—did Mrs. Martineau appear at tea. This consequently was dispensed by Martine in a small drawing room not much frequented except for the purpose. Many people, habituated to a great deal of space around them, never enter one room or another for weeks on end. The Martineaus, however, led an almost nomadic existence at Charne, so that if one visited there for only a short time one was apt to carry away the impression that one had seldom encountered one's hosts twice in the same spot. Judith Appleby had a theory— probably a perfectly valid one—that this slightly restless habit had been formed out of consideration for the servants, who might have considered it discouraging continually to dust, polish and burnish spaces and objects upon which their employers' glances or persons seldom reposed. Thus tomorrow at this hour Friary might be rounding people up with the murmured information that tea was being served in the Old Orangery. Appleby found himself already wondering whether the former Mrs. Gillingham would continue this odd expression of a social conscience.

Mrs. Gillingham was being attended to mainly by Bobby—Bobby's uncle appearing to be in no particular hurry to single her out for any more distinction than she might properly expect. Perhaps Bobby would really be indifferent to the bizarre plan conjectured to be getting under way at Charne. Perhaps he judged that an appearance of indifference would be politic. Perhaps he would fall for Mrs. Gillingham himself; she would make a very suitable maternal mistress—at least a dream one—for a young man of Bobby Angrave's mingled cleverness and emotional immaturity. Or yet again—and this was how one would develop the situation if one were writing a novel—Bobby would conduct an actual whirlwind courtship of the lady, and marry her while Grace Martineau's funeral baked meats were still on the board—thus thwarting his deceased aunt's shade. Having arrived at this not altogether agreeable fantasy, Appleby decided that he had better turn to thinking about something else.

"Bobby—do you see much of Dr. Fell?"

This sharp and sudden question from Charles Martineau diverted Appleby's mind effectively enough. It had occurred during a lull in conversation, and against a background only of the drinking of tea and the eating of tomato sandwiches—activities in themselves almost noiseless in polite society. Bobby Angrave appeared to find it surprising.

"Fell, Uncle Charles? I don't see him at all, except to pass the time of day when he visits here. Except once, that is, when I was staying with you last vac. I went over and consulted him about writer's cramp."

"Writer's cramp? Bobby would suffer from that!" Diana Page broke in with this; to scoff at Bobby was becoming rather compulsive with her. "I suppose it's what they call an occupational disease. You can't imagine Bobby catching a useful one—say, housemaid's knee."

"I'd read somewhere that writer's cramp is terribly psychosomatic, like stammering and bed-wetting." Bobby seemed to say this out of a sudden impulse to give mild offense. "So I went and saw Fell. He treated my sufferings lightly, I'm sorry to say. But why do you ask, Uncle Charles?"

Charles Martineau made no reply; instead, he preoccupied himself with picking up the plate of sandwiches and offering it somewhat at random to Mrs. Gillingham. Mrs. Gillingham, although she had moved on to a cake and was making little headway with it, accepted a sandwich at once. She was a tactful woman. She even shifted a little on her sofa, so that Martineau was constrained to sit down beside her.

"After lunch," she said, "I took a walk in the wood. It is most delightful, a great joy. And I found some Alpine Woundwort. I am sure you will have noticed it. Isn't it very rare—except perhaps in Denbighshire? At first, of course, one may mistake it for Wood Woundwort, which is common enough. But not at a second glance, because the bracteoles exceed the pedicels."

Charles Martineau received this with grave attention. He even found something to say about Field Woundwort, which was to be found near the river, just beyond the park. He hoped that Mrs. Gillingham would take a stroll with him in that direction, one day.

Appleby, although the Woundworts scarcely constituted one of his passions, had listened to this exchange with interest. It was his impression that Martineau was without any inner disposition to give Mrs. Gillingham a serious thought, one way or another. From this there appeared to follow the conclusion that if Grace Martineau really nourished the strange design which Martine imputed to her, she had not yet offered any hint of it to her husband. It was not a consciousness of that design, therefore, that could be the occasion in Martineau of some new species of anxiety which was to be sensed in him.

Appleby's feeling here seemed at first to make no sense. A dreadful cloud hung over Martineau's every hour, and if his sky now seemed even darker, the explanation must surely lie in a further lowering in the same direction. Yet this seemed not quite to fit. Martineau was much like a man freshly conscious of some lesser evil treading hard upon the heels of a greater. And Bobby Angrave was somehow involved in this; there had been an edge to that odd and inconsequent question about Fell that pointed to something of the sort. It was conceivable that Martineau had fallen into some sudden and morbid anxiety about his nephew's health—an attempted displacement of stress which would puzzle no psychologist. Certainly anything of the sort must surely be fanciful. Bobby, although he had the appearance of a sedentary creature, more at home with Greek particles than tennis balls, obviously enjoyed the rude and regardless health of his years.

You could look at Charles Martineau twice, Appleby reflected, without concluding yourself to be in the presence of anything out of the way; a standard sort of breeding and a standard sort of reticence appeared to sum him up. But his gentleness was a product of real sensibility. He was of a type to suffer acutely in and for others. It is something in which there is a kind of softness, Appleby told himself; a stoical man can be too little resistant to pain and unhappiness in those he loves—and the result is a personality not well tempered against some of the common exigencies of life.

"I wonder whether the nightingales will sing again tonight?" Martine asked. She turned to Mrs. Gillingham. "I am sure you will be interested in our nightingales, as well as in our toadstools."

"Toadstools?" It was naturally not without surprise that Mrs. Gillingham repeated the word.

"Weren't you speaking to Uncle Charles about toadstools? And so learnedly, we all thought."

This had the appearance of a declaration of war. Mrs. Gillingham didn't seem other than merely puzzled by it. But Charles Martineau was sufficiently attentive to be displeased—and this he expressed with a kind of gentle severity.

"Martine, dear, if you can't distinguish between *flora* and *fungi*, it will really be best that you don't embark upon botanical discussion."

"I'm so sorry." Martine was immediately graceful. "But what I meant to embark upon was ornithology—the nightingales. Or is it just one nightingale? Again, I'm

71

shockingly ignorant. Is the nightingale a solitary bird?"

"The poets—" Bobby began.

"Not the poets again, for goodness' sake!" It was, of course, Diana who broke in with this.

"It's my impression," Charles Martineau said, "that at present there are two male birds, although last night we heard only one. Perhaps we'll hear both tonight." He turned politely to Irene Pendleton. "But if you would like to hear a chorus of them, we could all drive over to Proby Copse. They haven't yet begun to be driven from there."

"That would be most delightful. Only this evening, Charles, let us be loyal to your own diminished band, whether solo or duet."

"Yes, indeed," Mrs. Gillingham corroborated. "Grace would like that best too. At lunchtime she was talking about the kingfishers."

"She loved the kingfishers." Charles Martineau's voice was not quite under control. "But as we were saying last night, they have taken their departure."

"But Grace has a plan." Mrs. Gillingham, having finished her cake, paused to make a token attack upon her second sandwich, so that something like a tiny current of suspense seemed to generate itself for a moment in the small drawing room. "It is for deepening the stream a little, and sanding it in some places, but with stretches of pebble and stone. Then it could be stocked with suitable small fish which are bred at a place somewhere in Gloucestershire. Grace gave me the name. And then, she thinks, the kingfishers may come back—although it may only be after a season or two."

There was a moment's silence.

"That is certainly to look splendidly ahead," Martine said. "If it ever happens, you must come back and see if it has been a success."

"Yes, indeed." Again it seemed to Appleby that Mrs. Gillingham was no more than puzzled.

"How sad," Bobby Angrave said, "that it is in the nature of plans to go wrong. Yes—how very, very sad."

Charles Martineau stirred uneasily.

"Diana," he said, "Martine and Bobby are tired of polite conversation. Take them away, please, and play croquet with them." Although his tone had been merely whimsical, the three young people, rather to Appleby's surprise, rose and obeyed like children. They went out through a French window, and their voices faded across the lawn. "And now," Martineau went on, "we have sacrificed the possibility of a game of our own! But I wonder whether you would care to walk round the rose garden?" He had addressed this question courteously to Mrs. Gillingham, so that to the others the invitation was no more than implied. "Grace will be joining us, I think, quite soon. And there are a number of things there that she would like to show you."

A moment later he was leading Mrs. Gillingham from the room. It was obvious that he had become aware of his nephew and niece as hostile to her. He was displeased—and, like Mrs. Gillingham herself, he was puzzled. Perhaps, Appleby thought, he wouldn't be puzzled for long. So far today, Grace Martineau had been husbanding her strength. It seemed not improbable that it was because she felt she had a big effort to make.

Chapter 9

SEARCHING HIS recollection of this evening shortly afterwards—and it was something he was rather grimly to be constrained to do—Appleby found himself recalling it as restless with a sense of obscure manoeuvre. The effect scarcely build up to the ominous—although retrospectively, and after the catastrophe, it was easy to imagine it as having done so. Charne was, of course, a place where a raised voice, an impatient tone, an ill-chosen phrase tended to reverberate—this simply because the house itself gave the impression of having been murmuring for generations that the paramount duty of its inhabitants was to consult the social ease of their fellows.

The game of croquet hadn't lasted long—which was, perhaps, not surprising, since it had only been begun more or less under orders. It is said to be an amusement that has a useful function in providing a harmless and ritual discharge of irritation and uncharitable feeling. Certainly it appeared to have given Bobby Angrave time to reflect. When he returned to his elders, it was to be quite as agreeable to Mrs. Gillingham as his uncle could have wished. Or—for that matter—his aunt. For Grace Martineau had now appeared—tranquil, and with the small clear stream of vitality that could still rise in her seeming to be running freely. It wasn't often, Appleby had noticed, that she looked at Bobby with any appearance of other than a strictly temperate pleasure. But his behaviour to Mrs. Gillingham plainly pleased her—or did so until it might almost have been described as getting out of hand. Bobby could hardly have been taken for one of the world's great lovers, but he was clever, handsome, probably sexually unscrupulous, and certainly possessed of a sufficient technique for putting these things across while remaining well within the boundaries of polite convention. If Mrs. Gillingham was puzzled—which seemed to be her role at Charne—she was certainly less offended than amused. When Bobby finally led her off gaily for a ramble in Charne Wood, it was almost possible to feel —quite scandalously—that the last thing they would presently be thinking of would be the subtle difference between one and another Woundwort. Appleby was sufficiently struck by this to carry his wife away to a corner of the garden on some botanical pretext of his own.

"Just what," he asked, "would you say that young Bobby is after?"

"He wants to annoy Martine. Martine believes herself to be considering at leisure whether, for the sake of possessing herself of Charne, she should put up with marrying Bobby. Bobby doesn't find being weighed up at all agreeable. So he has taken it into his head to show that, when he wants to, he can carry any woman off her feet." Judith glanced at Appleby suspiciously. "But I believe you want to unload yourself of a theory of your own."

"Bobby is going to thwart Grace's plan that Charles should marry Mrs. Gillingham by rapidly marrying her himself. Of course he will have to ditch Martine in the process."

"You think the woman would rather have Charne plus Bobby than Charne plus Charles?"

"It's possible. One might describe it as depending on her sexual constitution."

"But Grace would be furious."

"Grace might be dead before Bobby's counterplan was a week old." Appleby paused, frowning, in front of a mass of roses. "We have three more days at Charne, haven't we? I rather wish they were up. I know the Martineaus are very old friends. But all this seems to be distinctly their private affair."

"I think you're right. But you have begun scratching at it, you know, and you'll have to go on." Judith bent down to sniff at a rose. "So shall I give you one further fact?"

"Yes, do."

"Bobby wouldn't dream of marrying this Barbara Gillingham."

"That isn't a fact. It's an opinion."

"In that case it's a strong one. Bobby is very vain. He couldn't face being laughed at or smiled over as a young man in the tow of a matronly wife. Within five years he'd have a step-daughter who would look more of an age for him than his wife did. He wouldn't find that at all agreeable."

"Then my idea is nonsense?"

"Not at all. It may conceivably be well in the target area. Bobby needn't plan to marry the woman. All he has to do is to seduce her."

76

"God bless my soul! At Charne?"

"Why not? If he could do that, and deftly turn the occasion to open scandal, that would finish Mrs. Gillingham with Grace."

"If that's Master Bobby's idea, Master Bobby will have to hurry up. He must keep an eye on—well, call it Dr. Fell."

"Quite so. And perhaps bring it off—scandal and all —before it dawns on Mrs. Gillingham that she has a chance of Charles. If Mrs. Gillingham *has* a chance, that is to say. This plan of Grace's may be sheer invention on our part."

"I continue to bear an open mind as to that. Still, I do think we are excelling ourselves in rather gross imaginings. One can't suppose that now, at this moment, there in the wood—"

"Probably not—although I believe that such things are sometimes best achieved bang off like that."

"I think there's a flaw in the plausibility of your notion too. An improper affair with Bobby Angrave would certainly finish Mrs. Gillingham with Grace. But surely it would also finish Bobby with Charles. It would have been such an affront to Grace that he would never forgive the boy. It's not as if Bobby were a son, whom it would be unjust to exclude on the score even of some most reprehensible action. He's only a contender for favour."

"'I don't think I agree with that." Judith turned round, and they began to move back towards the rest of the party. "Even if not explicitly, Bobby is the acknowledged heir. He needn't do a thing, and Charne will be his in the fullness of time—apart from this supposed threat, that is, from the Gillingham woman. Once Grace is gone, and with that plan unachieved, it's inconceivable to me that there would ever be any question of Charles's marrying."

"Not even if Grace left a dying injunction that he was to do so, unaccompanied by pointing at Mrs. Gillingham or any other particular woman?"

"I think not. A second marriage will happen only if Grace pretty well joins this creature's hand to Charles's on her deathbed."

"You speak as if you rather dislike Mrs. Gillingham."

"I can't say I find her sympathetic. She's a little too much just that in a professional way."

"And that makes her a real threat to Bobby—and the final threat that the time element makes possible." Appleby stopped in his tracks. "Do you know that last night Bobby was calculating—quite inaccurately—that you could reckon to break somebody's neck by pitching him into one of those empty basins in the old garden?"

"I don't see—"

"What if we're slipping sedately into one of those well-bred English detective novels of the classical sort? *Death at Charne House.*"

"John, don't be absurd. Bobby Angrave wouldn't have the guts to murder anybody."

"Well, think of Martine as his fiendlike queen, egging him on. I'm not at all sure they aren't in some way really hand in glove. They're in a corner now, muttering about the dunnest smoke of hell, and that never shall sun that morrow see. It's just my luck."

"It's just your type of humour." Judith quickened her pace. "And in very poor taste, I'm bound to say. It comes of being embroiled all those years in low life and criminal practice."

"Actually, you have a much more macabre mind than I have. But of course I'm wrong. Bobby is still in the wood with Mrs. Gillingham. But not disrobing her tenderly amid the hogweed and the mosquitoes. On the contrary, he's holding her head under in that nice deep pool where you used to have fun with your pony. And I shall spend the rest of our visit being an embarrassment to the local police."

"John, do you know why you start up with this quaint sort of fun?"

"I don't know that I do. Perhaps it's just that there's a certain tension about the place at the moment."

"Yes—but it's a little more. It's a kind of natural magic. To *imagine* a thing is somehow to guard against its really happening. But of course it's all nonsense. There's going to be death at Charne, all right, but of the strictly natural order. . . . Look, Grace is beckoning to us."

They walked towards their hostess in silence.

"When I am dead," Mrs. Martineau said, "it is my wish that Charles should marry again. Shall we sit down?"

They had moved into the walled garden beyond the stables, and walked towards a westward-facing oval embrasure which held some garden furniture. Now they sat down without a word. The mellow brick behind them threw back its own heat towards the late afternoon sun. It was uncomfortably warm—but Grace Martineau still wore her enveloping shawl.

"It is something that I have wished to tell you—as I

have wished to tell Edward and Irene Pendleton too. It is my hope that you will all join together in sustaining Charles in his resolution."

"His resolution?" It was with a little difficulty that Appleby spoke at all. "Charles knows about this . . . this plan you have for him? He concurs?"

"Oh, no." Grace Martineau spoke calmly. "Not yet. It is my intention to speak to Charles later this evening. In the belvedere, perhaps—if it is one of my lucky times and I am able to take a walk there. . . . I think the nightingale will sing again tonight. And I want to hear it from the belvedere."

"Yes, of course." Appleby looked more closely at Mrs. Martineau than, just lately, he had cared to do. The only fresh impression he got was of intense physical suffering. This had its remissions, no doubt, or Grace would simply not be able to appear at all. But it must appallingly dominate what span of life she had left. And it would be easy, he thought, to feel in mere humanity that she ought to have no such span at all.

"And Mrs. Gillingham?" Judith asked steadily. "Does she know and concur?"

"Not yet. But, of course, I shall wish to tell Barbara too. She is very much younger than I am, and I have not seen a great deal of her of late. I hope you will like Barbara. She has calm and poise. Moreover, although the fact does not obtrude, she is deeply religious. I felt I wanted to have her beside me now."

This was baffling. And for Judith at least, who had decided not to approve of Mrs. Gillingham, it was uncomfortable as well. In such circumstances Judith was always likely to speak out. She did so now.

"You are inviting a confidence to which we must respond," she said. "Very well. I do not think that Mrs. Gillingham would be a good wife for Charles."

For a moment Grace Martineau received this only with a faint smile. Often now one had the impression that her mind was wandering—or even that it had just for some moments ceased to be there. This was natural enough. It was impossible not to suppose that she was rather heavily drugged.

"I love the sound of the bees," she said. "And this is the place to come and hear it. It is something to do with this curved brick wall. Their humming is richer and deeper—like a deep, deep sleep." She sank back in her chair. "One feels the air ought to be dark with them. And yet I think we have not so many as we used to have. . . . Judith, what were you saying about Barbara?"

"That I should not like to think of Charles as married to her."

Mrs. Martineau's faint smile had faded quickly, but now it returned again. She nodded her head—carefully, as if she had to calculate the amount of effort she could give to the motion.

"No, indeed," she said. "Barbara is an admirable woman, as I have said. But that wouldn't be a good idea, at all."

In the ensuing silence the Applebys looked at each other blankly. It was perhaps their first thought that Mrs. Martineau's intellect was really dissolving away. And then Appleby asked a question.

"You haven't, then, a specific person in mind when you speak of a wish that, one day, Charles should marry again?"

"But indeed I have!" There was surprise in Mrs. Martineau's voice—and also something like amusement at Appleby's being so far astray. "It is my wish that Charles should marry Martine."

Chapter 10

THIS TIME, the humming of the bees pointed a silence that was wholly stupefied. Judith was the first to recover.

"But Martine," she said gently, "is so very young! And, besides, she is Charles's niece—or at least your niece. I hardly think—"

"No, my dear—you are in error." Grace Martineau spoke calmly and clearly. "Perhaps you never knew, or perhaps you have merely forgotten. Martine was my dear sister's adoptive daughter. So nothing that the Bible says—if it *does* say anything about nieces—applies. Nor need there be any question of eugenic considerations. It is true that Martine, curiously enough, is a kinswoman of Charles's—but a very remote one. She was given the name of Martine, indeed, by way of honouring this distant connection with the Martineau family, which is of great antiquity and distinction. You must know that, Judith, being yourself connected with it as you are."

"These things are important to you," Appleby said.

"Yes, John, of course they are. The children—and there will be children—will be, by a small fraction, more than one-half Martineau blood. It is perhaps only a sick woman's fancy, but I do take additional satisfaction in that."

For a moment Appleby found no reply to this. It was very certain that a sick woman's fancy was operative at Charne in a larger sense than Grace Martineau asserted. Martine Rivière was no more likely to marry the elderly man she had always called her Uncle Charles than she was to marry the man in the moon. The idea was the merest cobweb. But whether there would be any kindness in trying to bring this home to Grace, Appleby found that he didn't know.

"I haven't yet told Martine," Grace went on calmly. "I think it best to speak to Charles first."

"I think that very wise," Judith said. She paused, and Appleby could see that she was thinking of the pain that this aberration in his dying wife would cause Charles Martineau. "But should it, perhaps, be given a little further thought before you suggest it to either? It seems such a fateful step."

"I have to think much in terms of fateful steps, my dear." With a surprising lightness—which could be felt, nevertheless, as the product of a huge effort of will— Grace Martineau got to her feet. "And now," she said, "I shall go to my room for a little time. We are a larger party than yesterday, and this evening we must be quite gay. I warn you, Judith, that I shall come down to dinner *en grande tenue*. You must tell Irene Pendleton. She would hate to be outshone."

Mrs. Martineau had moved away. Appleby sat down again with an expressive bump.

84

"Had we better do something?" he asked. "Speak to Charles?"

"Don't you think that perhaps Charles knows?"

"That he is to marry Martine?"

"No, of course not—not that. But that Grace's mind has come to move strangely, and that she may take anything into her head."

"I'm sure I don't know. But I do know that a bewildering variety of misconceptions are at this moment blowing about Charne. Grace, to put it mildly, believes that something inconceivable is both conceivable and desirable. Martine believes that Grace is plotting Charles's marriage to Mrs. Gillingham, and till a few minutes ago she had successfully infected us with the same baseless persuasion. Bobby Angrave seems to me to have the same notion—at which he may have arrived independently. Mrs. Gillingham may herself believe that she is in the running for Charles. Or equally she may believe that she is in the running for Bobby—and neither belief may be worth a farthing more than the other."

"Anything else?"

"Oh, certainly—although perhaps a little aside from this main imbroglio. Take poor Dr. Gregory Fell. He believes that I am interested in digging some past misfortune of his out of its obscurity. That's a misconception, too."

"Are you quite sure?"

"My dear, I might casually inquire, but I don't think I'd dig. Then there's Diana Page. She certainly believes that she scorns Bobby, and I rather suspect she sees that precious Friary as a kind of darkly romantic D. H. Lawrence proletarian lover. Two more illusions."

"Well, well! Apart from you and me, who of course never misconceive anything—"

"We don't—for long."

"—you've covered everybody. Or everybody except Edward and Irene Pendleton. Is there any misconception there?"

"They believe themselves to be wholly charming."

"My dear John!" There was real surprise in Judith's voice. "We have our little joke about Edward and Irene. But you don't often quite run to a crack like that. You're out of humour."

"Perhaps I am." Appleby rose, put out a hand to his wife, and hauled her to her feet. "Half-past six. It's almost time you were beginning to think of that *grande tenue* business too." For some moments they walked silently through the garden—a great warm walled space already heavy with the scents of evening. "I hate muddles and mysteries," Appleby said. "I like to know where I stand."

"And where other people stand too?"

"Exactly," Appleby said.

Appleby was conscious of reentering the house in an indecisive state of mind. It seemed certain that in a few hours' time Grace Martineau would lay her strange plan before her husband. Had he and Judith not been right in asking themselves whether Charles ought to be given some hint of it in advance? Charles, although he must be hoping against hope, had surely resigned himself by now to the knowledge that Grace would not be with him for much longer. But he probably believed that his mind and hers were closer together than they had ever been, and the alien thought which was in fact obsessing her might well come to him with all the shock of a virtual disintegration of prsonality suddenly perceived. The idea of his marrying Martine could scarcely strike him as other than gross and monstrous. So he ought, perhaps, to be perpared.

But who could do it? Appleby himself was an old enough friend, and it was possibly his duty to go straight to Charles now. On the other hand, it could be seen as a woman's task; he knew that Judith would do it if he gave the word; he knew, too, that she would carry it out rather better than he would. But—yet again—there was something to be said for giving such a painful disclosure what was surely its proper context of medical knowledge and experience, and Edward Pendleton—also a very old friend—could be relied on to exhibit the highest professional tact and expertness in such a case. It was quite certain, however, that Edward would decline the office—and for a reason itself professional and wholly unchallengeable. Grace was Dr. Fell's patient; it was Fell who must be making Charles, day by day, such reports on Grace's health as he thought fit; if something had to be said on her failing grip on reality it was Fell's prerogative to do so.

Having reflected on all this, Appleby found himself seeking out Charles Martineau at once. He told himself he was going to ask when Fell might next be expected at Charne; in his heart he rather supposed that he was himself going to plunge in straight away. For it was, after all, eminently the kind of event it is idle to think on too precisely.

Charles was in the room he liked to call his office: a

87

small apartment opening off the library, and itself lined with eighteenth-century books. On these shelves you would probably find a preponderance of sermons and forgotten historical and archaeological works. You would find too, no doubt, William—or was it John?—Halfpenny's *Rural Architecture in the Chinese Taste*. This inconsequent thought was in Appleby's head as he entered the room. Charles was at his desk, and just putting down the receiver of his telephone. Appleby took one glance at him, and at once concluded that the catastrophe had come —just a little earlier than everybody had expected. Charles was deathly pale. His whole body was trembling. The receiver had gone home with an uncontrolled clatter.

"Fell . . . is he here?" For the moment it was the only thing Appleby found to say.

"Fell?" It was almost meaninglessly that Charles Martineau seemed to repeat the word. He looked round the room as if unable to see where Appleby stood. Then he pulled himself upright. "I have been trying to get Dr. Robson," he said. "He is away from home."

"Dr. Robson?" Appleby now supposed that there had come no more than a sudden crisis—one in which a second medical opinion was urgently called for. "Grace is—?"

"Grace?" Charles spoke sharply, almost challengingly. "Grace has gone to her room to dress. She is looking forward to . . . to our dinner party. And Fell has been and gone. He has discharged himself from the case."

"Charles, pull yourself together. What you say is impossible. No doctor could do such a thing."

"It is true, John. I have behaved rashly, and can't forgive myself. It is this new and terrible anxiety. I taxed him with what must be the truth of the matter. He was very angry. It was not what I expected. He left the house in passion."

"Charles, I don't know what you are talking about. And I suspect some misunderstanding. Tell me, please."

Very strangely, Charles Martineau shook his head. He sank down in a chair. "No," he said. "I cannot enter into it. I cannot enter into this new thing now. We have known each other for a long time, John. Forgive me."

"Of course I mustn't press you. But just a little information might enable me to be of some help. Has this to do with something Edward Pendleton has thought it his duty to tell you?"

"Yes."

"And Fell lost control of himself—and you did too?"

"Yes."

"You told him you would call in this Dr. Robson?"

"No. I—I didn't get round to it." Charles produced this lame colloquialism with a moving helplessness. "John, what shall I do?"

"You need only calm yourself, I think. It won't be long before Fell—"

Appleby broke off sharply. There had been a knock at the door, and Friary was in the room. For a moment the man stood silent. He might have been waiting respectfully for permission to speak. But he carried again that rather ugly hint of dispassionate scrutiny of the scene revealed to him. Appleby found himself remembering the loggia, and Diana Page in tears.

"Yes, Friary?" Martineau had made a big effort, and his voice was level and unemotional. "What do you want?"

"A message from Dr. Fell, sir. He returned to give it. He asked me to make you his apologies—I presume for being called rather hastily away. I am to say that he will pay his usual late evening call upon Mrs. Martineau."

"Thank you, Friary. It was good of the doctor—but there was no need of it. Of course we expect him as usual."

"Quite so, sir. I am also to say that, at the same time, he would like a word with Mr. Angrave. And in your presence, sir. Those were Dr. Fell's words."

"Very well, Friary. You decanted the burgundy? It ought to breathe a little, I think."

"Yes, sir. The point has not escaped me. I hope that nothing does."

Friary gave his ghost of a bow, and withdrew. There was a prolonged silence.

"Charles," Appleby asked, "why do you keep on an insolent fellow like that?"

"Insolent?" Martineau seemed genuinely surprised. "Friary is an excellent man. There are irresponsible stories about him in the village, but I judge him to be completely trustworthy." Martineau rose from his chair. "We had better be getting along to change, John. And do forgive me, once more. In this last quarter of an hour there has been a good deal to forget." He smiled wanly, and touched Appleby on the arm to guide him to the door. "But at least Friary hasn't forgotten the burgundy."

"I look forward to it," Appleby said.

Chapter 11

IT WAS to seem to Appleby a curious feature of the affair at Charne that for just a little more than twenty-four hours after this enigmatical and painful scene in the small library almost nothing happened. At least if anything did happen, it failed to do so within the scope of Appleby's observation. After dinner, Charles and Grace Martineau made the little trip to the belvedere which they had planned—and presumably they heard the nightingale there, since the nightingale sang once more. But if Charles had indeed had to listen to his wife's strange proposal and been duly staggered, the only sign of it that appeared in him was perhaps the rather careful composure which he preserved among his guests during the short remainder of the evening.

This composure certainly extended to Charles's attitude to his nephew Bobby, whom he addressed with all his customary consideration. Bobby himself, on the other hand, appeared ruffled. Whether this was as a consequence of the proposed mysterious confrontation with Dr. Fell in the presence of his uncle didn't appear. What did appear was that he had abruptly lost interest in Mrs. Gillingham. Perhaps he had been rebuffed in some improper proposal advanced to her—although Appleby was inclined to think that this notion was the issue only of his own sustained professional acquaintance with human misconduct. Perhaps Bobby had somehow tumbled to the fact that Mrs. Gillingham was not the sort of threat it had been possible to suppose. However this might be, after dinner Bobby had given Diana Page a somewhat perfunctory invitation to get into his car and run round one or two pubs. Whether Diana would have liked to do this, it was impossible to say. She was certainly too well brought up to treat a tolerably formal party in this casual fashion, and Bobby had presently driven off alone. Appleby didn't know when he returned. Dr. Fell was certainly in the house shortly after Charles and Grace came slowly back from their small expedition. So perhaps Bobby and Fell met, after all.

It was at least certain that Martine could not have been presented with a sudden vision of herself as her Uncle Charles's preemptive bride. She had ceased, indeed, to be in any way challenging towards Mrs. Gillingham, but the only explanation required for this was, after all, that she had recovered her manners. To both the Martineaus her bearing was perfectly normal, and Appleby was convinced that she was not in the position of having to put any extra effort into this.

Amid this general calm it was only Edward Pendleton who appeared a little troubled. He was a man who, if he never positively relaxed—let alone unbuttoned— commonly presented the world with the most equable of faces. But now it might have been said of him, as of another weighty character, that on his front deliberation sat and public care. Appleby was far from disposed to make any inquiry into this. But, at the end of the evening, Pendleton sought him out of his own accord.

"My dear John," he said amiably, "I gather you have elicited from Charles some rather confidential matters which I felt bound to communicate to him earlier today."

"Scarcely that." Appleby wasn't too pleased with this manner of address. "I came upon Charles in a state of considerable agitation, and trying to contact a strange doctor. He told me that this chap Fell had walked out on his patient. I thought it most improbable, and I was right. Fell is back on the job. But there had been a flaming row. It wasn't very difficult for me to make the inference that you were at the bottom of it—if I may express myself in that way. And there my information ends."

"Yes, yes. It would be absurd in us to reproach each other, my dear fellow."

"I quite agree. And if I was curious at the time, it was simply out of an impulse to help Charles if I could. But he didn't want to discuss the matter, so that's that. And no more, Edward, have I broached it with you."

"Quite so, quite so." Pendleton was frowning indecisively. "I would like you to believe that I have been put in a peculiarly difficult position. You say Charles didn't pass on to you—?" Pendleton hesitated.

"What you felt you had to tell him? Definitely not. He said something to the effect that he couldn't bring himself to enter upon it."

"I see. I hope he didn't offend you by his reticence. But it is difficult—really very difficult. It would be idle in me to pretend now that I don't know something which must be admitted to this man's disadvantage. But here he is, respectably and legitimately employed in his profession. And I would stress *legitimately*. Moreover, I haven't the slightest reason to suppose that he is not a thoroughly competent G.P. And again, as far as Grace's case goes, I have made sure that he has been securing amply adequate advice from the best consultants. I would not myself have dreamt of saying a word to Charles—particularly, as you may imagine, at a juncture the nature of which must be only too clear to us all—but for something extremely disturbing which came to my notice only today. Even so, my dear John, I may well have committed an error of judgment."

Pendleton had produced this last reflection not without a detectable air of mentioning a circumstance wildly improbable. Having done so, and having—Appleby couldn't help feeling—elevated the whole matter to a suitable pitch of the mysterious—he now seemed to feel that this particular conference was concluded, and his own mind in some measure relieved.

"Dear me!" Pendleton said. "The household keeps early hours, does it not? But it is very understandable, of course. You and I had better be off to bed too."

"So we had." Appleby moved towards the door of the deserted music room—in which this conversation had been taking place. "By the way," he said casually, "would I be right in supposing that, at one time, our friend Fell was an anaesthetist?"

"Yes." Edward Pendleton not only gave this reply curtly; he swerved away from Appleby as he did so. "I'll just find those light switches," he said. "Don't wait for me, my dear fellow. Good night."

"Edward's attitude may seem odd," Appleby said, when reporting this interview to Judith a few minutes later. "But at least it's tolerably clear. He lays an information against Fell with Charles—I think that's the fair description of it—and then simply leaves the ball in Charles's court. As if Charles hadn't enough on his plate already."

"It's hard to believe that anything can be tolerably clear that produces such a muddle of metaphors." Judith, who was already in bed, put down the book she had been reading. "What's it all about, anyway?"

"I imagine that Fell may at some time have been in trouble with a professional body—the General Medical Council, or whatever—of which Edward was an august member. I imagine, too, that the trouble came to nothing —perhaps because of lack of evidence, or the like. But it meant a switch in Fell's career—a switch by no means for the better. And it has put him in the position of a suspected person. If trouble of a certain kind blows up in his neighbourhood, the police will make no bones about pulling him in and searching under his bed for housebreaking implements."

"Really housebreaking implements?"

"Don't be silly. Of course it would be a matter—at the start, at least—simply of unprofessional conduct. But eventually the police might arrive, all the same."

"But why does Edward simply shove this on poor Charles?"

"Because nothing was ever brought home to Fell, and it is really highly improper in Edward to breathe a word to Fell's disadvantage. At the same time, he feels his old friend Charles must be warned."

"The man's a menace."

"Fell?"

"He may be, for all I know. But I mean that Edward is. Coming at Charles with such stuff at this particular time."

"Quite so. As a matter of fact, Edward is making quite a to-do about the point himself. He calls it being in a peculiarly difficult position."

"Whatever Edward told Charles, I don't see why Charles need have had an immediate row with Fell because of it. Suppose that Fell has been at some time a confirmed alcoholic—"

"Or a drug addict."

"All right—that. If it's a thing of the past, and hasn't in any way interfered with Fell's professional skill in looking after Grace, I can't see why Charles, who's the gentlest of men—"

"I don't think I told you about Ronny Clandon and Tim Gorham." Appleby was now in pyjamas. "They're the key."

"Whoever are they?"

"Two young gentlemen resident in the county—or formerly resident in the county. Ronny has been put in a home. An even worse fate has befallen Tim. He's been sent to Australia."

"You certainly didn't tell me about them."

"I suppose I thought their story unedifying. They used to be a resource of Diana Page's when staying at Charne. And they were friends of Bobby's."

"They took drugs?" Judith asked.

"You're there in one. And what I think has happened is this. Edward has heard about these two unfortunate

96

young men—quite probably from Charles himself. And drug-taking, as Diana told me, is catching. When a little pocket of it turns up, it is natural for the parents of young people who have been on the fringes of it to get pretty alarmed. Indeed, they'd be fools if they didn't. Now Charles, who does easily get worried, may have been in this state of anxiety regarding Bobby, of whom he thinks the world. He may even have had good reason to be so."

"I can see Bobby having a go at drug-taking, but being very careful not to get hooked. He's a wary as well as a very intelligent young man."

"I quite agree. But now suppose that it is drugs that are in Fell's past. It probably is. Indeed, I asked Edward one question about Fell, which he answered. And he knew very well why I was asking it. Fell used to be an anaesthetist. As you know, it's the point of maximum exposure to temptation in the whole medical profession. Very well. Edward has been told that there has been drug-taking in Bobby Angrave's set—and then, quite unexpectedly, he discovers that it is Fell who is the local medical practitioner. He feels, absolutely rightly, that it is not his business to take any action on the strength of what can be no more than nebulous suspicion. At the same time, he feels that he has a duty to Charles, so he murmurs a word in his ear. Charles rather loses his head—for which one can't blame him at this time, poor chap—and comes out with something to Fell which obliges Fell to be very angry. And that, I imagine, is the whole story."

"And what do you think of it?"

"I don't want to think of it all. I don't want to be poking round Charne as if it was a kind of underworld. To be truthful, I'll be quite glad when it's time to go away."

"We can't possibly cut our visit short." Judith picked up her book again. "But I've arranged a kind of holiday for you tomorrow evening."

"A holiday?"

"You and I are going over to dinner with the Winstanleys at Clinton Amber."

"Who on earth are the Winstanleys, and where on earth is—"

"You know perfectly well that Hugo and Cynthia Winstanley are cousins of mine. You've met them several times. As for Clinton Amber—"

"It sounds most pretentious."

"It's nothing of the sort. And it's barely fifty miles away."

"Very well—but I suppose you've fixed this in a decent way with Grace?"

"Of course I have. She knows Hugo and Cynthia very well, and she wants news of them. She has that kind of feeling about people at present. She wants to gather them to her as she can."

"Yes." Appleby was silent for a moment. "But we oughtn't to arrive back too late."

"There will be no need to. Cynthia has promised to have dinner rather early. Do you approve of your holiday?"

"Yes," Appleby said. "I do."

Chapter 12

APPLEBY PUT in part of the following morning walking to the village to buy tobacco. It wasn't a particularly necessary expedition; he could well have waited until the excursion due to be undertaken later in the day. He simply felt that, for a short time at least, it might be tactful to keep out of Charles Martineau's way. On the previous evening, during the awkwardness over Dr. Fell, Charles had begged to be excused from explaining himself. Any uneasiness consequent upon this wasn't, perhaps, considerable; yet it existed, and was enhanced for Appleby by the fact that he had almost certainly pieced together the true facts of the case.

He wasn't, however, to take his walk in solitude. He had hardly entered Charne Wood—for he had decided to take that route—when Bobby Angrave appeared out of the trees and sauntered over to join him.

"Can I come too?" Bobby asked cheerfully, when Appleby had explained himself. "I really think I need some chewing gum—or perhaps it's a pair of shoelaces. Anyway, it's something that will take me outside this blessed ring fence for a bit. Shall we go on with our talk about death?"

"If you've discovered anything more that you think is improving to say on the subject, Bobby, of course it's my duty to listen. If not, not."

"It's not, then. And we must find something else. What about scientific medicine? That old buffer Pendleton—"

"Edward Pendleton is my exact contemporary."

"Yes, so I'd suppose—more or less." Bobby seemed unconscious of offence. "But, as I was going to say, Pendleton is always talking about scientific medicine. He seems to think it's a new kind."

"It's true in a way, I imagine. Far less in medical practice is merely empirical than was formerly the case. I'm not an authority."

"You must be an authority on forensic medicine—poisons and things."

"Of course I've had to know my way about." Appleby was rather amused. "But matters of that sort are often so intricate nowadays that one is very much in the hands of experts."

"What about drugs? I mean things like mescalin and Purple Hearts."

Appleby was silent for a moment. Then he decided that he wasn't going to concur in this sort of wary fishing.

"Bobby," he said, "what's in your head is that your uncle has been in some anxiety about such things."

"Perfectly true. Uncle Charles is a most extraordinary man. Think of worrying about that at this time." Bobby paused in his stride to glance at Appleby in a kind of horror. His mood seemed to have changed abruptly. "He's desperate, you know. I ran into him coming out of Aunt

Grace's room this morning. She was . . . well, moaning. And Uncle Charles looked like death. That's another thing about drugs—and it's really more terrible, to my mind, than all that bosh about young people turning into dope fiends wholesale. I mean how people can be kept alive on them. And ambulatory, if that's the word. Aunt Grace can be made presentable for hours on end—and then, it seems to me, she pays for it." Bobby, who was carrying a walking stick as was his rather elderly habit, took a vicious cut at a clump of hogweed. "She ought to be dead."

"About the other sort of drug-taking," Appleby said. "Have you done anything to relieve your uncle's mind?"

"Well, yes—of course I have." Bobby looked surprised. "But I'm not in a position to do so *tout court*. You see, when those chaps were mucking about with them, I did a little mucking in. It was uncommonly interesting, as a matter of fact."

"But you didn't get addicted?"

"Of course not!" Bobby's familiar contemptuous impatience flashed out. "I have some intelligence, after all."

"So had Coleridge and De Quincey."

"That's what my uncle said. But it's all nonsense. I exhausted the interest of the subject—and I'm still at large, and still in the hemisphere I was born in. But if you want to start inquiring where Ronny and Tim and the rest of that brainless crowd got the stuff, I'm afraid I can't tell you."

"I haven't the slightest intention of inquiring about anything of the sort."

"Oh, haven't you? I thought that might be why you started in on the subject." Bobby offered this quite idle perversion of fact as if it were a stroke of wit. Appleby failed to indicate amusement. They walked on in silence to the farther side of the wood, and dropped down into the village. "Let's go to the chemist's," Bobby said, "and buy up every grain of caffeine he has. I believe there's nothing to prevent us—and remarkable things can be done with it."

"Bobby, I think you ought to get away from Charne. It's doing you no good. It isn't even doing your blessed Latin prize poem any good, I imagine."

"Too true. And I'm sorry to be so absolutely filthy. . . . Well, here's the everything shop—tobacco, shoe-laces and all."

Bobby Angrave, however, made no further pretence of actually wanting shoelaces or anything. He remained outside the shop, and was still mooning around the little street when Appleby emerged.

"How interesting," he said, "that the top man in London's police smokes the kind of tobacco you can buy—" He broke off abruptly. "I say!" he said softly. "Look over there."

Opposite where they stood, and at right angles to the village street, a narrow lane ran between the gardens of a straggle of cottages. From one of these cottages the figure of a girl had emerged and moved hastily down the garden path. Now she had come through a little gate, and turned to fasten it. The movement had brought her directly in front of Bobby and Appleby, and at a distance which must have been less than thirty yards. It was Diana Page. She was looking straight at them—and quite blindly. It was to this strange appearance that Bobby's exclamation had drawn attention.

But there was much more to see—although the seeing, indeed, had to be done in an instant of time. For almost without a further pause, Diana had turned away and half-walked, half-run down the lane.

For a moment Appleby said nothing, and it was Bobby who first spoke again. "I've never seen Diana look like that," he said slowly. "And she must be in a queer state. She just didn't notice us." He laughed uncertainly. "She used to notice me a mile away." He looked uneasily at Appleby. "What was that expression?" he asked. "Fear?"

"I'd call it several things." Appleby spoke very soberly. "Shock and revulsion—and a lot of anger as well."

"It isn't the first time I've seen her poking about the village. I thought she was doing Aunt Grace's lady-of-the-manor stuff—taking soup to old women, and all that."

"She may have taken soup into that cottage. If she did, she has come away with something quite different." Appleby's tone was now grim. "Who lives in it?"

"Good Lord, I haven't a clue. I'm not all that the hopeful young heir, you know." As Bobby said this, he grinned rather feebly. The incident seemed to have upset him badly—even frightened him. "It must just be one rural character or another. Most of them are my uncle's people. Perhaps one of the foresters . . . Let's get back to the house."

"Very well," Appleby said. They turned and walked up the village street in silence. There was hardly anybody about. It was curious how much the place contrived to remain a village, even when a new and urban life was now only a couple of fields away.

"Do you know what I think?" Bobby Angrave spoke abruptly. "There's more going on at Charne than meets the eye—even the eye, perhaps, of that top London policeman."

"I agree," Appleby said.

"So what are you going to do about it?"

"Nothing whatever, Bobby. I see no reason to suppose that the hidden currents of which you speak have anything criminal about them. Even if they had, they would be no more my business than they would be yours, or any other private person's. Forget this top-policeman business, for heaven's sake."

"You disappoint me—or you would, if I believed you. By the way, you and Lady Appleby are going out to dinner, I think?"

"Yes—to some friends of Judith's at a place called Clinton Amber."

"The Winstanleys, that must be." Bobby Angrave brightened again. "Well, I'll keep an eye on things for you, while you're away."

"Thank you very much—but I haven't the slightest wish that you should do anything of the sort. I might be a private detective, hired to keep watch on your uncle's spoons and forks, to judge from your manner of talking. . . . Are we going to be late for lunch?"

"Heaven forbid. The punctual Friary would be most displeased with us. . . . I don't think I like that man."

"Your uncle regards him as most trustworthy."

"That's because my uncle is uncommonly trusting. One hates his ever being disillusioned."

"How does he behave when that does happen?"

"With severity." Bobby offered this seriously. "I think

you'll like the Winstanleys," he added inconsequently. "You'll find them restful."

"That may be."

"And even though you don't seem to want it—I promise you vigilance, meantime. Yes—I'll be your little Private Eye." Bobby Angrave was gay again. He tossed his stick in the air and caught it as he made this absurd remark. "You don't know what I shall report."

The moon had risen when the Applebys left Clinton Amber. It was another warm, near-midsummer night.

"Nice people," Appleby said. "I enjoyed meeting them."

"You mean that you enjoyed meeting them again."

"I assure you I didn't know them from Adam—or Adam and Eve. But Winstanley's an interesting man. I'm glad we went. It was a good idea."

"Thank you very much. And now—once more into the breach?"

"Oh, I wouldn't quite call it that—although Charne has been having its tiresome moments. Did I tell you how Bobby caught me on a walk into the village this morning? He talked some awful nonsense. But at the moment the place must be calm enough. They're sitting in the loggia; the nightingale is singing or not singing, as the case may be. Martine is remembering to be civil to Mrs. Gillingham. Bobby has wandered off and is mouthing Latin hexameters to himself. Grace will presently be going to bed, and Charles and Edward will be deciding to have a very short game of billiards. Another quiet day in the lives of the English landed gentry will have transacted itself."

"Well, that's something, I suppose. You've left out Diana."

"So I have." For a moment Appleby said nothing further. They had been driving down what was little more than a country lane, and he was bringing the car to a halt before joining a high road. "We'll be back in no time now," he said presently, as they gathered speed. "Diana Page? I'm sure I don't know about her. It's my guess that she's in rather deep water. But I'm blessed if I'm going to swim in it." Appleby frowned over the steering wheel. "Not that I'd have her drown, poor child."

"In fact, you'd swim for all you were worth." Judith glanced at her husband and laughed. "But nobody's going to get drowned."

"No doubt you're right. And the object of this little expedition was to get Charne in perspective, wasn't it?"

"Just that," Judith said.

The lodge gates were open when they reached Charne. Appleby drove through—and then suddenly checked his pace.

"Did somebody call out to us?" he asked.

"I don't think it was that. Drive on." Judith was looking back into the near-darkness. "The people in the west lodge are called Coombs. He used to be a forester. That was old Mrs. Coombs. She was staring as if we were the fire brigade. And she certainly exclaimed in one way or another. I expect she's a bit dottled, as my Scottish grandmother used to say. Charles keeps on all sorts of queer old people."

Appleby picked up speed again, and then slowed as he approached the sweep to the west of the house.

"Fell's car," he said. "He's a little later than usual. It's satisfactory that there's no more of that nonsense about Dr. Robson, or whatever his name was."

"Yes. Drop me, before putting the car away. I'd like to go straight up and say good night to Grace. She's usually fully conscious for half-an-hour, before something or other takes effect. She always reads Jane Austen. It's *Emma* at present."

"Very well." Appleby brought the car to a halt. "There's another car," he said. "And an ambulance."

Judith had opened the door beside her. But now she turned and for a second husband and wife looked at each other.

"I'll go and see," she said.

"Yes—and I'll get this car out of the way. There's been some emergency, I'm afraid."

As Appleby spoke, the west door of the house opened, and Bobby Angrave stood framed in it. He appeared to look out into the darkness, and identify the new arrivals. For a moment he turned round, as if speaking to somebody behind him. Then he came down the steps, and walked straight to the Applebys' car. He waited until Judith had climbed out.

"My aunt is dead," he said quietly.

"Oh, Bobby—I am so deeply sorry." Judith laid a hand on the young man's arm. "But we ought to be glad, perhaps."

"Perhaps."

"Can I go to your uncle?"

"No." Bobby Angrave shook his head slowly. "No . . . you can't. My uncle is dead too."

PART TWO

Friends and Relations

Chapter 13

A NOTABLE English novelist—one bearing, indeed, the highest of contemporary names—has exhibited Muddle as the archenemy of human happiness. It is certainly the archenemy of Commissioners of Metropolitan Police. It is the archenemy, for that matter, of any policeman who finds himself with a sudden press of human testimony on his hands. Mr. X's car has an unfortunate brush with Miss Y's bicycle; Mrs. Z—on the pavement, shopping basket in hand—has been ideally circumstanced to look on. But confusion is immediate, and is presently enhanced by young Master A—who steps forward (out of series, one may say), school satchel on back, too young to be relied on (except covertly) by the magistrate, but plainly to be given some credence by anybody really concerned to arrive at the truth. Everybody wants to be honest; everybody, in one degree or another, is frightened; the conflict of voices thus generated has to be heard to be believed.

In *Death at Charne House* it wouldn't be at all like this. The dramatis personae would advance one by one, each in turn under the spotlight—a mild sort of spotlight, by no means glaring pitilessly into the contracted pupils of wretches successively under interrogation. The only penetrating beam would lie in the level gaze of the person—Great Detective or humble sergeant of police—charged with the business of presently rendering all lucid to the sleepy reader curled up in bed.

Sir John Appleby knew that at Charne matters weren't going to be conducted after this fashion. He was to be confronted by Muddle—and Muddle that was none of his business. He was—it was idle to deny—the authority in exigencies of the kind that had blown up; long ago he had sorted out such affairs in St. Anthony's College, in Scamnum Court, in the rat-ridden castle of Erchany, far up the Parana (had it been?) where they kept the calculating horse and the disassociated girl, even on that wholly deplorable Pacific island known for some reason as Ararat. It was natural that people should gape at him now—or should do so, at least, as soon as it was acknowledged that something more than simple fatality had occurred. But he didn't like it. He had traffic problems to get back to, and the wickedly disinherited children they called Mods and Rockers, and disgusting pockets of indecency organized to collect ten-pound notes from business gentlemen, impeccably, chapel-going in Preston or Hull, who unfortunately found themselves at large for an evening in London's West End. This was Appleby's world—quite a serious world, quite enough to be going on with. And now he found himself conferring with a bewildered local constabulary in the country house of an old friend—an old friend just deceased.

The police had actually arrived. Dr. Fell had declared—pretty well on the instant—that they must be sent for.

They were in the music room, being regaled by Holman Hunt's Shakespearian musicians with ditties of no tone.

Musing among these masterpieces, Appleby looked broodingly at Christopher Sly. He was, for some reason, compelled by Christopher Sly—perhaps because that sadly bewildered tinker had a natural right to be considered the presiding genius of the present gathering. For bewilderment is just what happens when your host and hostess both die on you. Nobody knows who ought to give this quite trivial direction or that. And the absurdity of such small social dubieties throws into relief the stark fact of mortality.

One looks, oddly enough, for a chief mourner—for only upon him, or her, can the beginnings of a composing social ritual be built. It was Bobby Angrave, rather than Martine Rivière, who seemed to fill the bill. Bobby's controlled reception of Appleby and Judith must have been the product of a stiff exercise of the will. It looked as if the young man's legs had ceased to be useful to him now; he was limp in a chair, intermittently his whole body trembled.

If an opposite extreme were to be sought, it would be found in Friary. Friary—quite incredibly, but simply because it was his prescriptive task at this hour—was dispensing drinks. No longer having an employer to consult, he had decided off his own bat that the two uniformed officers of police should be included in this dispensation. He received with evident disfavour their somewhat abrupt indication that thus to join in the household's compotations would not be at all in order. Not that anybody else, for that matter, was accepting drinks. Or nobody except Mrs. Gillingham. She had allowed herself to be provided with a glass of barley water. It was clear that at Charne nothing at all in the nature of a wake was likely to get under way.

"This is deeply distressing—most deeply distressing." Edward Pendleton had come up to Appleby with this remark. His tone couldn't quite justly have been called perfunctory, but his manner clearly intimated a conviction that it was time the two Top People on the scene began to pull together. "Of course when it has been a matter of firearms, these fellows have to be called in. They will be required to give evidence before the coroner, and so on. But these are mere wretched formalities. Can't you get them away, my dear fellow, and leave us to our grief?"

"Certainly not. They must be their own judges of what is necessary. I have no standing in the matter whatever."

"They don't look to me likely to make much headway. I'd say they were a bit overborne by their company."

"If they are, it's no credit to us. Still, there's some sense in what you say, Edward. We need someone who won't even be conscious that he's standing up to the gentry. That's why I've stretched a point."

"Excellent, my dear John. You mean you'll take hold of this thing yourself?"

"Definitely not. I'm in precisely the position that you are—or Friary there. But I've advised them to get through to their station and get the fellow in charge to contact the Chief Constable."

"I see." Edward Pendleton was dubious. "Isn't that to make rather a thing of it?"

"It may possibly turn out to *be* a thing—without any making on our part."

"I'm sure you know best, my dear chap. Charne's in the county, I imagine, and not the borough?"

"Certainly it is."

"You know this Chief Constable? He's—?" Pendleton paused significantly.

"He's a Colonel Morrison." Appleby was conscious of a need for patience. "And not late-risen from the people, or anything disagreeable of that sort."

"My dear John, if there's anything I can't be charged with, it's being a snob. But there are times when one doesn't want too many jumped-up fellows running around."

Appleby found no reply to this—or no reply of any particular relevance.

"I began on the beat myself, you know," he said.

"Ah, yes—but of course that was rather different." Edward Pendleton evinced mild disquiet; he clearly felt that Appleby had said something that wasn't very good form. "Well, I must go and comfort Irene a little. Naturally, she's very upset, indeed."

Pendleton moved away abruptly. It was what Appleby had designed that he should do. He himself was only a spectator, as he had said. But at least he wanted to see clearly. He would sit down in a corner—there was nothing else to be done—and piece together what he knew so far. It wasn't much.

Hard upon the death of his wife, Charles Martineau had gone into his office and killed himself. So much Bobby Angrave had conveyed to Appleby at once, but thereafter the general shock and confusion still predominant in the household had much impeded the flow of fur-

115

ther information. Had Appleby felt himself to be in charge, he could no doubt have assembled in ten minutes such preliminary facts as there were. But to be a spectator merely and not involved as a player or in the action, he had to await what the general disorganization cast up to him. The first odd circumstance, perhaps, consisted in what was reported about the conduct of Friary. It was Friary who had heard the shot—or rather who had alone heard it for what it was, and with distinct attention. Other people thought that perhaps they had heard it, or that at least they had heard something like it. They explained how this had occasioned no alarm. The popping of firearms was not encouraged round Charne, but even outside the shooting season there was a certain amount of it. Grace Martineau's notion of wild nature was such, one gathered, that Charles's keepers had discreetly to thin out sundry predators if its appearance was to be preserved.

Friary had heard the sound for what it was: a pistol shot within the house. And Friary—now so composedly offering unwanted whisky to all and sundry—had apparently panicked. Instead, that is to say, of going straight into his master's office, he had rushed around the house shouting for help. Edward Pendleton had already murmured that there was nothing surprising in this; the fellow had never been in the army; servants are unaccountable at all times. Appleby, on the other hand, felt that if he himself were minded to be curious he would probably start being curious at this point. He had gathered something of Friary's private interests; there was nothing very out of the way about them; but Appleby had often had occasion to remark that professional amorists are a bit soft. Friary by no means struck him, however, as nervously flabby. If the man behaved oddly, it would be because he was under considerable pressure of one sort or another.

But now, at least, everybody had some excuse for being in a state of shock. In a sort of delayed reaction, the double fatality was coming home to them. A thousand deaths are not ten times as appalling as a hundred—not by a long way. If there were a machine to measure such things, it might show, correspondingly, that two deaths fall at least some way short of being twice as appalling as one. There can be circumstances in which duality suggests positive comfort—as when a childless and devoted married couple die simultaneously in a road accident. Some sense of this sort might even have been conjectured as likely to obtain in the present case. But Charles Martineau hadn't died beside his wife; he had died after being agonizingly parted from her. Nor—and this added to the sense of horror which was beginning rather mysteriously to pervade the matter—had he died the same sort of death. Charles had died, one might say, by fire. His wife had died by water.

Chapter 14

IT HAD REQUIRED a little time for Appleby to arrive even at this quite simple fact. He had taken it for granted—the moment Bobby Angrave spoke, he had taken it for granted—that Grace Martineau had died, if not in her bed, then at least on the way to it. And when the truth—the first bare fact of it—had come to him, it was of Bobby Angrave that he found himself thinking: Bobby standing by one of the great stone basins in the obliterated formal garden, and proposing to fill it to the brim as a surprise for his uncle. But the basins, of course, were still dry. It wasn't in one of these that Grace had been found drowned. It was in that deep pool in Charne Wood through which Judith Appleby had once proposed to urge her pony.

That a man should, by his own hand, follow his wife to the grave is a solemn and dreadful thing. But if it is to be condemned it must be either on religious grounds or in terms of some humanist persuasion that we best show our devotion to the dead by continuing in a state in which we can remember and honour them.

Appleby, turning this over in his mind as he sat alone for a little in a corner of the music room, had a sense that he wasn't quite wasting his time. What these thoughts had brought him was a suspicion that a little professional activity might be incumbent upon him, after all. But, if it were, it wouldn't be at all a matter of his duty as a policeman. He had, of course, a duty to keep the Queen's peace and protect the Queen's lieges. The Queen, after all, might be said to have done very well by him, so that he had a particular obligation to do as well as he could by her. Yet these very proper considerations, he knew, were very far from likely to set him breathing down the neck of Colonel Morrison and his men. What he was seeing now, however, was that he conceivably had a duty to the Martineaus. Their death mustn't be got wrong. In all probability there was no hazard of its being so. It all seemed simple—and sad—enough. But the simplicity was, in one aspect, so painful a simplicity that it ought to be tested before being accepted. It ought to be tested hard.

Appleby's first test was by way of Judith, and took place shortly after they had gone finally to their room.

"Grace is as well where she is," he said. "And perhaps that goes for Charles, too. Looking at the thing now, one sees the utter nonsense of Charles married to Mrs. Gillingham, or Charles married to Martine."

"Oh, quite. It doesn't mean that Charles ought to have blown his brains out—if it was his brains."

"Certainly it was his brains—and *very* out. That sort of action has a shocking aspect of sheer physical mess."

"Yes, of course." Judith had been sufficiently involved in certain episodes in her husband's career to take this in her stride. "I'm going to begin *Emma* tonight. I brought up a copy from downstairs."

"*Emma?*"

"Grace had got to the place where Emma doesn't repent her condescension in going to the Coles."

"I see." It must often have been in an extremity of pain that Grace Martineau had followed for the last time the fortunes of Miss Woodhouse and Mr. Knightley. The small private commemorative act now proposed by Judith would have pleased her. "Are you left puzzled by anything in this affair?"

"Yes." Judith gave this reply at once.

"Just how is it mysterious?"

"It's mysterious—if ever so slightly—in your simple Scotland Yard way. Weren't we making a stupid joke about *The Mysterious Affair at Charne,* or something of the sort? I've sometimes thought it fatuous to get excited about this particular death or that as being mysterious, when every death there ever was is a mystery there are absolutely no clues to."

"Yes," Appleby said patiently. When Judith offered remarks of this kind of philosophic generality, it usually meant that she was getting something quite different clear in her head.

"Charles acted out of character. The puzzle lies there. What are the reasons why people commit suicide? You must have them all indexed in your head."

"Not all, I imagine—but a good many of them. Some people do it rationally—almost, you might say, on a hedonistic calculus—when they realize that their bodies have finally betrayed them, and that there is nothing left for them except pain on this side of the grave. For in-

120

stance, if Grace had drowned herself deliberately, instead of by accident—"

"Yes, of course. What about the other reasons for suicide?"

"It can be done by way of punishing people by whom one believes oneself to have been slighted. 'They'll be sorry now.' That's quite common."

"Yes?"

"Melancholia—the real, black thing."

"Yes?"

"To cheat an insurance company, to avoid imprisonment or disgrace intolerable to one's pride, to rate half a column in one's local paper or two or three lines in a national one—" Appleby broke off. "And, of course, by way of self-punishment and expiation."

"Would that be it?"

"It seems the only way of getting round your feeling that Charles acted out of character. Of course, the facts are still obscure. But there was Grace, wandering alone in Charne Wood—"

"Tottering alone. Wouldn't that be more accurate?"

"Yes, it would. And Charles may have felt that he had been unpardonably careless. He may have shot himself in some access of remorse."

"Do you think they'd been making another of their little trips to the belvedere? The other evening, Grace said—"

"Yes, I remember." Appleby nodded. "She said something about their sometimes coming away together and sometimes separately—just to show they could still be independent of one another. I scarcely thought her serious."

"They may have been in the belvedere, and she may have challenged him, in some way, with that rather high-spirited air she had. He may have given in, against his better judgment, and left her there. Then she set out on her small, independent return—and it was the end of her. Charles would blame himself bitterly."

"Certainly he would." Appleby thought for a moment. "But not to the extent of shooting himself. It still doesn't make sense."

"Very well." Judith was now sitting in front of her dressing table, apparently intent upon dispassionate scrutiny of what its looking glass revealed. "In that case, we have to go deeper. He must have wished her dead, you know."

"Isn't that a little crudely put?"

"We're confronting something crude. Crude or cruel. It's the same word, I believe."

"I agree that of late there must have been times when Charles could have felt that Grace's life was intolerable to her, and that it would be very merciful if she might die. But he can scarcely have believed, say, that he left her to make her own way back from the belvedere as the result of some subliminal prompting to put her life in hazard. That she should turn faint—or whatever actually happened—just at the moment and in the posture that would take her into that pool was a chance that no unconscious mind would gamble on."

"Yes, but that's not the point—or not the whole point. In times of great emotional stress our minds are said— aren't they?—to function in pretty primitive ways. Unconsciously perhaps, we believe, for instance, in the independent reality of our thoughts; in their power to go out from us and do things. That's why we go into mourning. We imagine—"

"But we don't go into mourning." Appleby felt that he really had to object to this one. "Not any longer."

"Well, it's most unhealthy not to. We mourn, in one way or another, to punish ourselves for the lethal thing our own thoughts have achieved."

"Yes, I know. Or rather, I don't know, because I suspect it's really most awful rot. You're saying that poor Charles nourished an unacknowledged death-wish against his wife, even if it was on what may be called respectable compassionate grounds. So when she did die, and die by misadventure, he succumbed to a bit of primitive magic, acknowledged to himself he'd killed her, and then took his own life in order to even things up. It may be so—but why not imagine something simpler? All we're looking for is some sudden additional stress or strain that would quite knock Charles off balance for a while. His wife is dying. Then, suddenly, along comes something else."

"You mean a worry about Bobby Angrave, or something?"

"No, not that. For the moment, I put anything of that sort aside. It must be a something else that has to do with Grace directly. Why shouldn't it be the crazy marriage business? Suppose it was only tonight that Grace broached that. And suppose that, as a result of it, Charles and Grace quarrelled."

"They couldn't quarrel." Judith was shaking her head vigorously. "Not at that stage in Grace's illness. It's inconceivable."

"In a sense, it takes only one to make a quarrel. And the stage of Grace's illness, with her at least, might predispose to some nervous explosion. Charles would almost certainly be horrified and revolted by her strange fancy. He might betray his feeling. And a quarrel—call it a lovers' quarrel—might result. Charles would walk away, if only to cool off. And never see his wife again. Their last words would have been spoken in anger—and only because of a plan of hers which she believed to be for his good. When this came home to Charles, hard upon the news of Grace's death, he really might, I believe, have made away with himself."

This last suggestion of Appleby's produced silence for a time. Judith had got into bed, and now she picked up Jane Austen's *Emma*. But she could hardly have been reminded that the novel's heroine was the younger of the two daughters of a most affectionate, indulgent father, before she spoke again.

"John, isn't there another possibility?"

"There are probably dozens."

"Mayn't Charles have taken his own life because Grace took her own life?"

Appleby, who was placing a pair of shoes where he hoped they would catch the eye of a doubtless distracted housemaid in the morning, turned round and stared at his wife.

"Grace! You think it was no accident?"

"Why should it be? People don't much fall into deep pools they are perfectly familiar with—not even when mortally ill. But the pool might have had its attractions for Grace. Didn't she say something to us about deep, deep sleep? Well, it's a deep, deep pool."

"People sometimes throw themselves off a bridge, or into the ocean. But they don't just lie down—"

124

"Yes, they do. Shelley did. He just lay down in quite a shallow pool, and stayed put."

"He didn't drown."

"There was somebody there to pull him out. But, seriously, a woman might be drawn to take her own life in just that way. Indeed, I can think of one very distinguished woman who did."

"And Grace did—and Charles knew?"

"I don't know." Judith picked up *Emma* again. "It's just one more way it may have happened."

Chapter 15

IN THE PAGODA room—named from an ancient and gorgeous wallpaper and used only for the consumption of breakfast—Mrs. Gillingham was discussing a frugal cup of coffee and studying a road-map. She looked up as Judith entered, and a shaft of early sunshine caught her perfectly ordered hair.

"Good morning," she said. "I hope that the sideboard carries what you require. Friary is usually in attendance, but today he has neither appeared nor sent a substitute. Perhaps he is still upset. He will certainly be glad to see us go." For a moment Mrs. Gillingham's glance went back to her map. "One has almost to regard him as the head of the household."

"You are leaving at once?" Judith asked.

"It seems the proper thing to do. As it happens, I am on a round of visits." It was without self-consciousness that Mrs. Gillingham made this rather old-world pronouncement. "There is a slight awkwardness. However, I have sent a telegram, and everything is arranged."

"I'm so glad." It occurred to Judith that Mrs. Gillingham, so restful in restful times, showed up as a shade chilly against Charne's new background.

"One's farewells are a little tricky. I shall say good-bye, of course, to both Bobby and Martine—but perhaps to Martine first. Writing afterwards is a different matter."

"You mean a bread-and-butter letter?" Judith found the social problem thus propounded decidedly odd.

"Exactly. To whom shall it go? One must, after all, continue to observe the forms. Fail in that, and chaos is come again." Mrs. Gillingham, although she spoke with a faint irony, seemed to mean what she said.

"Perhaps the problem isn't an immediate one. Perhaps we shall be asked to stay."

"My dear Lady Appleby, what an odd idea! Bobby and Martine, I imagine, will want the house—or should one say an arena?—to themselves."

"No doubt. I certainly don't suppose that they will be very pressing. I was thinking of the police."

"The police!" Mrs. Gillingham was startled. "Do you mean Sir John?"

"Of course I don't. I mean the Chief Constable, who appears to have arrived at dawn. It's true that John has seen him. I have no details, and don't seek any. But it appears there is some new doubt about the manner of Grace's death. She may have met with foul play."

"Then that explains the absence of Friary. The Chief Constable has produced a pair of handcuffs and haled the unhappy man off to jail. I wonder whether they gave him time to put on that very superior dustcoat."

It was Judith's turn to be startled. She helped herself to coffee, and sat down.

"I really don't understand," she said. "Why should Friary be suspected of anything?"

"Because he had earned Grace's displeasure. Not that that is other than a very mild way to put it. To speak seriously, Lady Appleby, there is something that I would like your husband to know."

"The police, I think, would be—"

"No doubt. But I have been put in rather an awkward position, and I am anxious that Sir John should be the first to know about it. He may judge the whole incident to be irrelevant. So may I trespass on your kindness? Tell him briefly what I have to say. If he thinks it important, he must speak to me."

"Very well." Judith felt that she could not do other than agree. But she was not wholly pleased. "Why should there be an awkwardness?" she asked.

"I find I cannot acquit myself of a charge of eavesdropping. Or rather of spying, since little was audible to me."

"I see." Judith didn't, in fact, see why Mrs. Gillingham should think the vindication of nice feelings of particular importance in face of what had happened at Charne. "When did this occur?"

"Yesterday afternoon. But I ought to say, first, that since my arrival at Charne on this occasion I have been conscious of a peculiar atmosphere, and of this as somehow particularly affecting myself. Martine's manner to me has been very peculiar."

"Martine believed that Grace was planning that you should marry Charles." Judith wasn't sure why she came out roundly with this. Perhaps it was merely to startle the decidedly cool Barbara Gillingham. She hoped that it was prompted by a more reputable feeling that, in the present circumstances, there was a strong case for candour all round. "And I think Bobby," she went on, "may have had the same notion."

That Mrs. Gillingham was indeed startled it would have been impossible to deny. Perhaps—it suddenly came to Judith—Grace's supposed plan had veritably been Mrs. Gillingham's own plan. Perhaps, at least, she had not been without a thought of Charles Martineau in his approaching widowerhood. But she certainly hadn't supposed such a project to be lurking in any other head. Now she spoke with gravity and dignity.

"Had Grace formed such a wish," she said, "she would have told me. We were old friends enough."

"I am sure that is true. And Grace had no such wish."

"You know that positively?" This time it was with a sudden sharpness that Mrs. Gillingham spoke.

"I think I can say that." Judith had come rather abruptly to a point at which candour had better stop off. To speak about Grace's strangely revealed thought of Martine as a possible successor seemed unnecessary and meddlesome. "But what is the relevance of this to what we were speaking of?"

"Ah, Friary. I had been made slightly uneasy about feeling towards me here—that is what I was saying—and this may have made me act a little oddly. It was yesterday afternoon, and Grace was sitting by herself in the orangery. I was about to join her from the terrace, when I saw that she was extremely agitated. I ought to have gone to her at once, since it would have been the intimate and kindly thing to do. But for some reason I hesitated. Then I saw her pick up the telephone—you know how Charles had these things put all through the house for her—and summon somebody. I withdrew to the little recessed seat—you must know it—at the corner of the terrace. One of the parlourmaids came, and Grace spoke to her very briefly. I think the maid—it was the one called Evans—was surprised by her mistress's condition. She went away, and then Friary came instead."

"You continued watching?"

"Yes. I ought, of course, to have moved away. One's friends' dealings with their servants are decidedly not one's affair."

"I'm sure that is a very good rule. And then?"

"Grace upbraided him. It was a most painful scene."

"It couldn't just have been over some domestic negligence?"

"No, indeed. That could not be the explanation. The thing had quite a different quality."

"Very sick people—"

"That is true. I understand what you mean. But no. Not that."

Judith was silent. She had no disposition to think that Mrs. Gillingham was talking nonsense.

"And that is all," Mrs. Gillingham said.

"Of course nobody else saw this?"

"Naturally not."

"But how did it end?"

"Friary simply came away. He came out into the open air—which was odd in itself—and walked down the terrace and round to the back of the house."

"Without seeing you?"

"Certainly without seeing me. For the moment, he was past seeing anything. He looked very pale. I am bound to say that I thought he looked very evil as well."

After this curious interview with Mrs. Gillingham, Judith obeyed an impulse to get into the open air. As soon as she stepped out on the terrace, she ran into Martine Rivière. And Martine stopped and spoke abruptly.

"Judith—have you heard the news?"

"I've heard of a possibility the police now feel they must investigate." Judith looked curiously at Martine. She was no longer the composed young woman that she had appeared to remain the night before. "I don't know that we do much good speculating about it ourselves."

"But that's nonsense. If there is such an incredible suspicion, we can scarcely be expected to keep our minds on other things and make suitable small talk when we meet."

"That is true. But we must remember that, when a thing like this happens, it becomes the duty of the police to consider every possible interpretation. So we don't want to start talking about it on the basis of supposing the worst. To do so might be to inflict wounds that would prove hard to heal."

"They say there were marks on Aunt Grace's body! It's incredible."

"Nearly incredible—which is just my point."

"Yesterday—quite suddenly—there was something between Aunt Grace and Uncle Charles." Martine had gone on unheeding. "That's one thing that makes it too awful."

"You mean they had some dispute or estrangement?"

"It seemed like that. And it can only have been about

that woman."

"I think it may have been about a woman. But of what woman are you thinking?"

"What woman?" Martine looked at Judith queerly. "Barbara Gillingham, of course."

"I don't think so." Once more, Judith was suddenly prompted to clear at least one further area of confusion. "But what is in your mind, Martine?"

"My aunt had decided that Uncle Charles must marry the woman."

"It isn't so—although both you and Bobby may both be convinced of it. Your aunt had decided that your Uncle Charles should marry you."

"I don't believe it!" The words came from Martine like a cry, and she had gone very pale.

"I'm sorry. But I think it is something that should be known—at least to yourself. And you mustn't be too shocked. Grace thought the world of you. She wanted children at Charne. And she believed—I suppose rightly —that there was no legal or moral impediment. I can see that the idea is bound to offend you. It must have offended your uncle, if it was really communicated to him. But you must remember, as I'm sure he would have done, that a dying person can see things very strangely."

"She didn't like Bobby. Uncle Charles did." Martine came out with this as if inconsequently. And then she paused, with an effect of gathering in its relevance. "Of course you know that Uncle Charles had a matchmaking plan of his own. He wanted me to marry Bobby—which would be something perfectly suitable and proper in itself, I suppose. With that in his head, he could hardly have received Aunt Grace's idea as other than a joke. The more one thinks of it all, the more grotesque it seems. Old people ought not to be ambitious to arrange marriages. They just don't know what's absurd."

"I'm sure you are right, Martine. If I ever feel the ambition myself, I shall restrain it."

"Diana too, you know."

"Diana?"

"Yes—Aunt Grace's notion again, this time. She thought of Diana for Bobby. She thought that Diana would *do* for Bobby."

"You mean—?"

"Yes—that Diana would be quite good enough for *him*. It wasn't a very good basis upon which to promote a match. And it was hardly kind to Diana."

"Not if she let Diana know that she looked at it in just that way."

"Oh, I'm sure Aunt Grace would not do that." Martine seemed really shocked. "Certainly not intentionally. And Aunt Grace was too sensitive, surely, to let such a thing slip in an inadvertent way. But at least she must be said to have put ideas in Diana's head."

"And to no purpose? It wouldn't be something Bobby himself would think of?"

"Bobby might think of anything. He is unaccountable. I don't understand him." Martine said this abruptly, and for a moment seemed to be about to break off the conversation. Then she thought better of this. "But you know how Bobby and Diana are always sparring at each other? Aunt Grace was struck by it. She seems to have taken it as a sort of technique of courtship."

"I'd say that it is that, in a way. Or at least it is on Diana's side."

"Oh, yes." Martine was suddenly contemptuous. "Diana has been after him, and my poor aunt is to blame. I think—although I don't really know—that Diana is a mess."

"But surely you and Diana are close friends?"

"Yes. Or that's the idea. Or we were." Martine was frowning in some obscure perplexity. "Everything has been all wrong. And out of it, somehow, there has come this horror. Policemen saying that Aunt Grace has been murdered. Perhaps, by this time, they are saying the same thing about Uncle Charles as well."

"Martine, I must insist that the police are not even saying anything of the sort about your aunt. They have only a suspicion. I'm a little surprised, actually, that they seem to have let it get around."

"Oh, that must be Sir John, you know."

"John?" Judith was sharply angry. "That is nonsense."

"I don't think so. He is the expert, after all. And he wants to rattle us." Martine paused. It was impossible to tell whether she believed what she was saying. "His first success has been with Diana. Diana is terrified."

Chapter 16

IT WAS ONLY a few minutes later that Martine Rivière's last statement was borne out somewhat dramatically—almost, indeed, to the effect of another sudden death at Charne. Judith Appleby, going in search of her husband, and rounding a corner of the house in some absence of mind, was recalled to her surroundings by a screech of brakes in her ears and the appearance of a car bonnet pretty well under her nose. Automatically she had taken evasive action; now she stepped back a further pace and took stock of what had happened. The car—small, by no means old, but carrying the suggestion of being miscellaneously battered—was Diana's. Diana was at the wheel, and she seemed to be aware that she had been behaving dangerously. But, although she contrived to produce some sort of apology, she didn't switch off her engine.

"Heavens, Diana—you do seem in a hurry! Where are you off to?" The question wasn't really necessary. The back of the little car was piled with suitcases and a heap of loose clothes.

"I have to leave. I've been called away. Isn't it a frightful bore? But it can't be helped." Diana's manner was as wild as her driving had been. She was confused, frightened, and obeying a simple impulse to bolt.

"That seems a great pity." Judith walked up to the car, and put a hand on one of its doors. "Have you told people?"

"Yes . . . no. There hasn't been time. It's illness in my family, and terribly urgent. Good-bye."

"Diana—that isn't quite true, is it? You just want to go away because things here have been distressing you? I don't think you should. Not without talking to somebody."

"I don't want to talk to anybody. I talked to Mrs. Martineau. And you see what happened."

"Diana, whatever do you mean by that?"

"Nothing. I didn't mean to say anything. That's what I'm *saying*, isn't it? So leave me alone. Let me drive on."

"If you want to, then of course." Judith took her hand from the door of the car, and stepped back a pace. "But it won't be any good. I think I ought to tell you that."

"What do you mean—it won't be any good?" Diana sounded uncertain. "You're trying to frighten me."

"That isn't so, Diana. You are frightened already—and you'll go on being frightened till you face up to things. When I say it's no good bolting, I mean simply that you will be visited wherever you go, and asked questions. And that isn't unreasonable. You see, it's just possible a crime may have been committed at Charne—"

"Of course a crime has been committed." Diana's voice had risen in panic. "I just don't want to get killed too."

136

"I don't think that's at all likely."

"Yes, it is. He may kill anybody."

"Diana, what do you mean? Who may kill anybody?"

"I don't know. I don't know what you're talking about. Let me go." Diana Page was now reduced to a condition of childish incoherence. It wasn't easy to see her as other than rather a rubbishing little person, and Judith reflected that Grace Martineau's estimate of her nephew Bobby's worth must have been decidedly low if she had really felt that in Diana Page he would find a suitable wife. This didn't mean that Diana must be harshly treated now. The child was desperately in need of support—and in need, too, of somebody to confess to. This last impression had been with Judith for some time. But now, if Diana was not talking utterly at random, there seemed a real need to extract sense out of her. Judith tried a fresh line.

"Diana," she asked, "does Bobby know how upset you are?"

"Bobby? Bobby wouldn't ever know anything. He wouldn't ever notice anything—except his own beastly silly cleverness!" Diana was now in tears—tears that were angry and unbeautiful. "And *she* seemed so clever —so clever and wise and kind. I believed her. Don't you see?"

Judith did see, and her feeling of compassion for Diana grew.

"She was," she said. "Or she used to be. But I think, Diana, that her illness clouded her judgment. Her illness and some other wishes that she had."

"Other wishes! What other wishes?"

"Never mind that now. And I am so sorry. You were

terribly disappointed when Bobby turned out not to be interested after all?"

"I could have taken it." Diana had raised her chin, so that a tiny flicker of spirit seemed to appear in her. "But he had his fun with me."

Judith said nothing. It wasn't a point at which to make a mistake.

"I've put that stupidly. He didn't shove me into bed. Perhaps he just hasn't got what it takes." Diana was suddenly vicious.

"He flirted with you, you mean?"

"What a funny word. You make it sound like something in a novel. But yes, I suppose so. He chatted me up. He could get me all excited without touching me. And then he'd go away laughing."

"I see." Judith found that this picture of Bobby Angrave as a pretty average young cad failed to surprise her. "And then you rather lost your head?"

"I suppose so." Diana looked straight at Judith in sudden defiance. "In fact I lost more than that."

There was a moment's silence. Judith had a sense of Diana's last words as not, somehow, ringing quite true. In a witness box Diana would cut an unimpressive figure. Was she a vicious child, or a child who had been gravely wronged? A jury would resent not being able to make up their mind about her.

"And so, you see, it has all been my fault." Diana's tone had suddenly changed again. "I didn't mean to do anything wrong. In fact, I thought for once that I was doing what was entirely right. But it was a mistake, wasn't it? Because Mrs. Martineau was murdered. And perhaps Mr. Martineau was murdered too. I wasn't, because he thought I'd be too scared to speak. But now I am speaking. And I suppose I'll have to go on."

"Yes, I think you will." Judith felt a sudden enhanced sympathy for Diana, who seemed really to be on the way to overcoming some vivid, if irrational, fear. "You have said things that make it certain the police will want to take a statement from you. So I think—"

"Couldn't I tell Sir John?"

"Yes, I think you could. At first, at least—if you would prefer it that way. Shall I ask him? I'm going to look for him now."

"Yes, please."

"Then go and put your car away," Judith said quietly. "And get at least some of these things back to your room."

"But we'll all be able to leave Charne soon?"

"Yes, of course, Diana. And there's nothing to be afraid of."

"Wasn't that Diana?"

Judith, crossing the terrace, turned round as the voice spoke—peremptorily rather than politely—just behind her. It was Bobby Angrave who had appeared so abruptly. Thus confronted, Judith allowed herself a moment's silence.

"Sorry, Lady Appleby. With something like this on our hands, one does tend to forget—wouldn't you say? —what that Gillingham woman calls the forms. But it was Diana, wasn't it?"

"Yes."

"What was she doing, fooling around like that in her car? It seemed piled up with luggage."

"Diana had decided to go away. I had to dissuade her—although I'm not sure I wanted to." Judith paused. "She hasn't had a very good time at Charne."

"My dear Lady Appleby, who has?" Bobby said this with a decently subdued amusement. In contrast with the previous night, he seemed confident and relaxed. The way he had said "My dear Lady Appleby" seemed in itself significant; the tone was that of one remembering simultaneously both his juniority and his status as a host.

"It's a trying time for everybody, no doubt." Judith began to move forward again, since she felt no prompting to conversation with Bobby at the moment. "Can you tell me where I shall find my husband?"

"Yes, I think I can." Bobby had fallen in beside Judith in a manner that was now wholly courteous. "He's with this Colonel Morrison in Charne Wood. They've established a kind of headquarters in the belvedere, and now they're planning an arrest. I suppose you know who is going to get arrested?"

"No," Judith said, a little shortly. "I don't."

"I am. I don't think there's a doubt of it. Not after the latest development. I shall be in jail before nightfall. But I'm told one can have meals sent in."

Judith said nothing. This was the kind of nonsense, she reflected, that Bobby Angrave was accustomed to talk when in high spirits. It seemed decidedly inappropriate that he should be in high spirits now.

"Perhaps," Bobby said, "you just haven't *heard* of the latest development?" He looked at Judith challengingly, and almost as if piqued by her lack of interest. "There's been activity in my uncle's office, you know. All the resources of science, and so forth. Men in heavy boots and blue serge suits taking photographs and discovering fingerprints. I particularly like the fingerprint business. Do you know? It's done by puffing powder everywhere, and then blowing it away. Just as in one of those two-and-sixpenny paperbacks."

"Bobby, all this is upsetting, of course. But I don't see why you need let it release a spate of flippant talk. You don't amuse me—not a bit."

"I'm frightfully sorry, Lady Appleby." If Bobby's was faintly a mock penitence, it was at least without insolence. "You see, I'm scared stiff. The notion that Aunt Grace had been deliberately drowned by someone was pretty horrible—but at least it seemed to have no immediate practical meaning. Martine says Aunt Grace may have discovered something about a servant, who lost her head—or his head—and killed her. It's revolting, thought of like that, but it doesn't touch us. Just a nasty irruption from belowstairs. Edward Pendleton would see it that way."

"So he would," Judith said—and at once regretted that she had encouraged this talk by a single word. But Bobby's last remark had been perceptive enough.

"But there's no doubt what they're gunning for now. Take, for example, the gun."

"The gun?"

"The gun that fired the bullet that killed Uncle Charles. It was Uncle Charles's gun. There's no question of that. He kept it, ready loaded, in a drawer in that damned room. Nobody knows why. I heard Sir John tell this chap Morrison—the Chief Constable, you know—

that quite a lot of people do something of the sort. Arrested development and boyhood dreams of the Wild West. Or some quite unconscious prompting to suicide. Or the more or less rational feeling that a man of property should be able to defend his possessions until the Dicks turn up. But the point is that the photographers and the fingerprint chaps have been having a field day with it. You understand? A clever murderer could fake that sort of suicide easily enough. But he might make some tiny error that these blue-serge characters could spot if they were clever enough. And now all that's going on." Bobby paused in this torrent of speech. "It's horrid, of course. But there's a kind of morbid excitement in it."

"There seems to be."

"Particularly for me. Perhaps for Martine too, in lesser degree. As yet, we know nothing about the wills, and so forth. Martine had her prospects. But mine were the big ones."

"Bobby, ought you really to be talking like this? It's rubbish, but I rather resent it, all the same. These deaths are not matter for idle wit. Anything of the sort can only seem hysterical and rather silly. But I suppose I must tell my husband what you've been saying. Or this Colonel Morrison, who is of course the man in charge."

"Tell them both." Bobby Angrave, who was carrying his customary walking stick, flung this in air and caught it deftly as it came circling down. "Don't you see? These two people—my uncle and aunt—stand between me and a great inheritance. And suddenly I'm in a fix with them. I needn't tell you about that now; it will emerge soon enough. And, straight away, both come to a violent end." Bobby stopped in his tracks. It appeared to be his intention to accompany Judith no further. "I'm sorry," he said. "Frightfully bad form, and all that. But you'll see that I have to keep my spirits up. And I'm not likely to do that by retiring into a summerhouse and writing bad Latin verse."

PART THREE

Heirs and Assigns

Chapter 17

"On the back of the neck," Colonel Morrison said. "Our surgeon is a very reliable man. And now he's had his opposite number out from the town. This fellow Pendleton too. He seems such a bigwig that it seemed civil to ask him. He stipulated that he wouldn't be required to give evidence to the coroner. Perfectly right and proper, that. Of course if it came to a criminal trial, it would be another matter."

"And Pendleton concurs?" Appleby asked. The two men were standing on the podium of the belvedere. "He suspects violence?"

"Yes. But what worries me, you know, is that it doesn't make sense."

"Murder, you mean, in a place like this?"

"I mean nothing of the sort. Crime may turn up anywhere." Colonel Morrison chuckled grimly. "Sorry," he said. "Teaching you your business, eh? I keep on forgetting."

"The more you do that, the happier I shall be. I'm not out for a busman's holiday."

"Of course not. But you won't withhold your advice, all the same." Morrison was silent for a moment. "What I meant was something quite different," he went on. "Why grab the old lady by the neck and leave your marks on her? Why present the police with the slightest hint of violence? Everybody about this place must have known Mrs. Martineau's physical condition. Once in that pool, she hadn't a chance. All that was needed—granted she could be got to the edge of it—was a shove. Nothing more."

"I see your point." Appleby found himself taking mental note of the fact that Morrison was a man worth working with. "But one has always to remember the irrational state in which even contrived and cold-blooded crimes of violence are actually committed. And this crime—if it *was* a crime—may not even have been like that. . . . What about robbery, by the way?"

"She was wearing some quite valuable jewelry. She could have been reckoned on as doing so, at that after-dinner hour. But it was there when they fished her out."

"A bag?"

"That was fished out too. Nothing much in it. Nor would one expect much. Women don't carry wads of banknotes on an evening stroll."

"A woman might be carrying an incriminating document."

"Perfectly true. Or she might be carrying a key to the Kremlin's top cipher of the moment. One must rule nothing out."

"Neither about Grace Martineau nor about her husband."

"I quite agree." Morrison glanced swiftly at Appleby.

"The fellow's own weapon. In his hand, and without any prints other than his. Discharged at close range into his right temple. Hence that quite ghastly mess."

"Quite so."

"But access is the important point. And there it is: actually three doors to that small room. We've got to face it. Anybody without an alibi might have possessed himself of the gun beforehand, walked in, killed Martineau, fixed things as they were found, and walked out again—all within sixty seconds. Lucky that chaps don't get round to murdering each other all that often, wouldn't you say? It's too damned easy."

"The clock is the important thing, in this case. Who was where when—and with whom."

"Yes, indeed. And the Applebys have an alibi." Morrison paused broodingly. "If you and Lady Appleby hadn't gone out to dinner, you know, this might never have happened. Nobody would have had the nerve. Homicide, or double homicide, under the nose of the Commissioner of Metropolitan Police. Think of it!"

"I wasn't all that far away. And I can imagine somebody seeing the virtual presence of such a personage as a challenge. But what about that clock?"

"Ah!" Colonel Morrison's exclamation was one of satisfaction. Perhaps he felt that he had hooked his man. "Would you like my chaps to come with their notebooks, or will you trust me to have got it pretty clear in my head?"

"Not chaps with notebooks, please. Go ahead." Appleby sat down on a broad stone step. "Nicely warmed by the sun," he said. "Won't do even the elderly any great mischief."

"If you're prepared to risk it, so am I." Morrison sat down too. "And here goes."

"Ten P.M.," Morrison said. "It has just struck on the stable clock here at Charne. The summer solstice. A clear sky. Even in Charne Wood you can see your way clearly. Macaulay and his nephew have no difficulty."

"I don't know them," Appleby said. This dramatic style of narration on the part of the Chief Constable had taken him by surprise. Then he remembered. "Is that the name of the head gardener?"

"Yes. A most respectable man, it seems, who has been about the place for a long time. And his nephew—actually a grand-nephew—has lately arrived from Aberdeen to be one of his assistants. They are returning from some occasion in the village. The servants, it seems, like everybody else, use one or another of the paths through the wood."

"So they do. The butler does."

"The butler? Ah, yes—Friary. I've a note on *him*." Morrison paused. "Well, these two come on Mrs. Martineau's body. It wasn't totally submerged, you know. A leg caught in something overhanging the bank. They haul her out, and Macaulay is convinced she is dead. Unfortunately he says so—before sending his nephew hurrying down to the house for help. He himself starts some thoroughly efficient attempt at artificial respiration. He was in the Black Watch in the Kaiser's War. Sound chap."

"And then?"

"The nephew—he's called Neil Something-or-Other—came rushing out of the wood, and found Charles

150

Martineau alone on the terrace. *Everybody* was alone, you know. That's part of the devil of it."

"Except Macaulay of the Black Watch and nephew Neil."

"Yes, yes. The boy told Martineau that his wife had been drowned. He's only a lad, you see, and that's what he blurted out. Martineau seemed stupefied. He cried out 'Where?'—just like the fellow in some play or other." Morrison paused. "Funny thing—I can't remember which."

"*Hamlet*—and it's what Laertes asks about Ophelia." Appleby had seen that it was necessary to supply this information before Morrison would go on. "And then?"

"The poor devil recovered a bit, and did get out of Neil that Macaulay was with Mrs. Martineau and doing what he could. At that, Martineau turned and ran into the house."

"And ran to his death?"

"Almost instantly. Nobody can be found who saw him alive again. Five minutes later—or it might have been ten—Friary came into the music room in a panic. At least I suppose he was in a panic. There was nobody in the room except the niece, Martine Somebody—"

"Rivière."

"Thank you. Miss Rivière was there, playing the piano—"

"Something noisy?"

"It's a point, Appleby. We must find out. Well, Friary behaved with no more control than young Neil. He stuttered out something about a pistol shot in the master's office. And at that—"

"One moment. Suppose that Friary did really hear the shot—by which I mean merely hear it, and not fire it as well. Is it certain that he ran *straight* to the music room?"

"I don't think it is. In fact I have a notion that he put in a minute, or thereabout, blundering around. And I see what you're after. It's perfectly true. Miss Rivière herself could have made the music room before him—and started banging out Beethoven or whatever. But the whole damned household is in the same boat. And the design of the house—or at least of the ground floor—is a kind of dream setting for this sort of thing. Several routes from any one point to any other."

"Oh, quite so." Appleby had already reflected upon this point. "And then?"

"I was going to say that Miss Rivière wasted no time on this wretched Friary. She jumped up and made for Martineau's office. In the hall she heard a click of balls from the billiard room, and knew that it was her cousin —the young man called Andover, or some such name."

"Angrave. Bobby Angrave."

"That's right. I don't care for him—but that's by the way. Miss Rivière called to him, and they both ran through the library, where they picked up this top surgeon, Pendleton. And then the three of them went in and found the body. And that's the whole story. At that point, you may say, our investigation begins."

"But we have to go back a bit, don't we?" Appleby had got to his feet again. Leaning against a pillar, he was staring absently at the closed door of the belvedere. "You rang the curtain up at ten P.M. But what about before that?"

"Yes, indeed. Well, my impression is that they were all behaving a bit oddly, you know, for what you'd reckon to be a tolerably sociable hour of the day. Young people, of course, have simply ceased from civilized living. But in a place like this you'd surely expect—" Colonel Morrison shook his head and broke off gloomily.

"I know what you mean. But life hasn't been quite normal at Charne just of late. Remember that Mrs. Martineau was a very sick woman indeed."

"And other strains and stresses too, eh?"

"Well, yes. Indeed, we'll have to come to them. Related strains and stresses. Marriages and inheritances. That sort of thing."

"I thought so." Morrison nodded sagely. "So many wheels within wheels in this place, if you ask me, that one can pretty well hear the damned things whirring all the time."

"That puts it quite admirably. But how did things go after dinner?"

"That's certainly a good point at which to begin again, and get the hang of this unsociable scatter I was speaking of. Do you know, Appleby, that even the butler scatters?"

"Friary?" Appleby sat down again, laughing. "Yes, indeed. He's supposed to go off to the village for a modest pint. For my own part, I'd distrust a beer-drinking butler."

"I certainly distrust Friary. But the first point is that, quite soon after dinner, the Martineaus strolled away together. It's something, it seems, that was becoming a habit with them."

"They used to come up to this little temple—it's called

a belvedere—in their early days. The small trip was a sort of continuation of their wedding journey, I'd say. Which is why—"

"I quite see." Morrison appeared to find this sufficiently uncomfortable to want to cut it short. "Well, up they came—or so one has to suppose—and that, once more, is the end of the matter. The next direct sight of either of them is of Mrs. Martineau already dead, and of Martineau himself staggering under the news young Neil brought to him."

"But what about Friary—whether we trust him or not? We were talking about the clock. Well, Friary *was* a clock. It was the Martineaus' own word for him. He would pass here—just down there, below us—on his way back from the village, with the precision of an ocean liner picking up a light at its precise moment. Or so we're asked to believe."

"Yes, I've got that. And the fellow *did* pass—and saw nothing and heard nothing. At least we're asked to believe that too."

"Any inquiries made about him in the village yet?"

"Give us a chance, my dear fellow!" Colonel Morrison was suddenly plaintive. "We're not, you know, one of your flying squads."

"Of course not. But it occurs to me that you and I might take a stroll there now."

"To the village?" Getting obediently to his feet, Morrison allowed himself a brief stare of surprise. "I'm in your hands."

"And here's my wife, coming up through the wood. I expect she'll join us. Do you mind?"

"I'll be delighted, I need hardly say." Morrison's enthusiasm was detectably of the surface. "We need all the help we can get."

"Well, yes. And Judith, as a matter of fact, has rather a knack of picking things up. I shouldn't be surprised if she had something to tell us now."

"There's plenty to think about in all that," Colonel Morrison said ten minutes later. He had listened to Judith in silence as they continued their walk through Charne Wood. Now he turned to Appleby. "It would certainly seem that a little investigation in the village is in order. But how would you say that we organize things after that?"

"Begin with the least sinister hypothesis. More often than not, in affairs of this sort, it turns out to be the true one. Grace Martineau was accidentally drowned; her husband was heartbroken, and shot himself. Against that, there are the marks as of violence on Mrs. Martineau's neck. You say they're only such as to occasion suspicion."

"Strong suspicion."

"Yes—but I've heard of that before. And the body of an elderly woman can be bruised easily, and in odd ways. But of course there is other evidence we have to consider. The thing takes place in a general context of what one may call lurking motives and obscure predicaments. So go on to the next least sinister hypothesis, so to speak, and review matters in the light of it."

"I'm blessed if I quite know what that is. One crime rather than two?"

"Just that."

"Very well. It's conceivable that Mrs. Martineau died by accident and that her husband was murdered. Or vice versa. I'll choose vice versa. That means that somebody wants to kill the lady, but has no ill design—or effects no ill design—against Martineau himself."

"Charles Martineau may just have been too quick," Judith said. "He may have killed himself before somebody else, so to speak, could do the job for him."

"The brain reels." Colonel Morrison produced this with some faint design upon a humorous note. "But we'll say, for a start, that Mrs. Martineau was the only destined victim. Yes"—he kept up his attempt—"we'll pursue our quiet rural walk thinking about that. Which of all these people, Lady Appleby, would you say comes to mind?"

"Oh—Mrs. Gillingham, decidedly."

"God bless my soul!" Morrison gave Appleby a glance of alarm. He might have been reflecting that it must be pretty tough even for a Commissioner of Police for the City of London to have a wife with a mind which worked like this. "Is that what they call the least-likely-suspect theory?"

"Not at all." Judith shook her head briskly. "Mrs Martineau was cherishing a plan that her husband should make a second marriage with Miss Rivière. But Miss Rivière believed—and so did the young man Bobby Angrave—that Mrs. Martineau's choice had fallen on Mrs. Gillingham herself. This may have penetrated to Mrs. Gillingham—she strikes me as a very astute person—and put ideas in her head. She'd get rid of Mrs. Martineau before Mrs. Martineau could push her own plan further, and then she'd get to work on the widower on her own behalf."

"I see." This notion kept Morrison silent for a dozen

paces. "But isn't that rather monstrous?" he asked. "For you don't mean, surely, that this widowed Gillingham woman had developed some violent sexual passion for Martineau?"

"I should judge that most improbable."

"Very well, my dear lady. Surely no sane woman does another woman to death in the interest of an elderly and tranquil union with a husband thus bereaved? Or is Mrs. Gillingham to be conceived of as in some state of financial desperation?"

"I suppose she might be—although one sees absolutely no sign of it."

"My wife," Appleby said mildly, "takes rather a dark view of Mrs. Gillingham. But you will find her—for professional purposes, that is—prepared to take an equally dark view of almost anyone."

"Oh, I'm sure she is." Morrison, who was a little at sea, produced this with an air of compliment. "But here we are," he went on, more happily. "Here's the village; there's the village shop; and those, I suppose, are the cottages. Appleby, you know the one we're after?"

"Definitely. It's the one with the honeysuckle by the door. But I hardly think, you know, that we should all crowd in."

"Of course not. And it's a delicate matter, if our guess is right." He turned to Judith. "Lady Appleby, would it be asking too much—?"

"I wasn't supposing otherwise," Judith said, a shade tartly. "John, go and buy more of that evil-smelling tobacco, and take Colonel Morrison with you."

Judith walked away, and the two men stood for a moment, watching her go.

"My dear fellow," Morrison murmured, "your wife's a remarkable woman. If I may say so without impertinence, that is." He pointed to the village shop. "It's the post office too, I see, and sure to be a centre of intelligence. No harm in asking a question or two, eh? The whole place must be alive with gossip by now."

"It must, indeed," Appleby said.

Chapter 18

THE VILLAGE of Charne ended in a roundabout. To that point the buses from the city came, and only a couple of hundred yards short of it did they disengage themselves from the outermost of the municipal housing estates. But from the roundabout, so far, only a cul-de-sac ran into Charne itself—and this gave it its precarious and residual tranquillity. In exterior semblance it was more of a model village than was, perhaps, altogether agreeable to a picturesque taste, since in the late nineteenth century some well-meaning Martineau had knocked down a great many worm-eaten cottages and rat-infested hovels, and erected several uniform rows of dwellings, suitable for the labouring poor, instead. The work had been well and generously done, so that the inhabitants considered themselves commodiously catered for down to the present day. But the general effect was utilitarian. Nobody would want to stand at gaze with it for very long.

Appleby and Morrison, having bought their tobacco and made their inquiries, had certainly exhausted the interest of the scene by the time that Judith returned to them. She came to a halt and looked at them seriously. She might almost be said to have looked at them sternly and wonderingly, as if confronted by an alien species. And Morrison—Appleby noted—saw the explanation of this at once.

"Lady Appleby," he said, "it's as we thought?"

"Yes. And just short of fourteen."

"And so far," Appleby asked, "they've kept quiet—the parents, or whoever they are?"

"Yes. It's unbelievable. It's dismally feudal. They think of it as trouble with the big house, and are reduced to a kind of frightened cunning. Yet Charles must have been the most just of landlords and most conscientious of squires."

"The first thing this calls for is a telephone message to Dr. Fell, I'd suppose." Appleby's tone was grim. "I'll make it from the kiosk outside the post office. It won't take me three minutes. After that, I've a fancy for going back to the belvedere. As yet, I've hardly looked at it." He walked away.

"At least," Colonel Morrison said to Judith, "this has nothing to do with Mrs. Gillingham. And it does bring us up against a straightforward and provable crime."

"That is something, no doubt."

"What is your own impression of this fellow Friary?"

"The man's a blackguard."

"What happened to the Martineaus quite apart, it seems to be heading us for rather a nasty scandal. Not good for the county, that sort of thing."

"I suppose not."

"But at least we can get the fellow jugged. 'Carnal knowledge' is the beastly phrase for it. Do you think he's actually seduced this girl at Charne—Diana Somebody —too?"

"Diana Page. I doubt it—but he may have. She was badly thrown off balance when she discovered that Bobby Angrave had no real interest in her."

"And Friary may have got her in the family way as well?"

"That's more improbable still. But one never knows."

"Such things happen, certainly. And a horrid mess it would be."

"It would be no worse for Diana, Colonel Morrison, than it is for the bewildered child in that cottage."

"Of course not. But the fellow must be a fool, among other things. You're sure that Miss Page discovered what has happened to the child, and took the story to Mrs. Martineau?"

"There can't be a doubt of it. And Mrs. Martineau tackled Friary."

"And where does this lead us? That's the question." Morrison paused, frowning. "This Page girl didn't strike me as having much stuffing. Am I right?"

"Quite right. She's been trying to bolt."

"Suppose she has herself really been badly entangled with Friary. And then suppose Mrs. Martineau, to whom she has alone confided her discovery here in the village so far, to die a mysterious death. Would it be a good bet that Miss Page would be so frightened that she wouldn't utter a further word to anyone?"

"I think so. She'd just want to run away from Charne, and never see any of us again."

"Then there you are. But here's your husband." Morrison turned to Appleby as he came up. "Lady Appleby and I have elevated Friary to the position of chief suspect."

"It's rather a stiff rise. Still, if we're considering a crime, or crimes, committed from a motive of fear, Friary is distinctly in the running. If we think of the motive as greed, on the other hand, then Judith has found a useful outsider in Mrs. Gillingham."

"And would you say there is a favourite?" Morrison asked.

"Good Lord, yes. Viewed that way on, Bobby Angrave is in a class by himself. And then comes his cousin Martine. They give us the direction in which the property is presumably to go."

"It would be useful to have some certainty about that."

"Decidedly it would. And about some other things as well. But now, as I said, I want to have a look at the belvedere. And another look at Charles's office, after that."

"And then have a word with people?" It was almost casually that Morrison asked this.

"If you want me to, yes."

"Good. I'd like to see this damned mystery cleared up before the day's out."

"That's a challenge, I suppose." Appleby reflected for a moment. "Do you know—I think I'll take you on?"

As they approached the belvedere, somebody came out of it. It was Friary. He gave the three approaching figures a swift glance, and began to walk away.

"One moment, Friary." It was Appleby who called out briskly. He waited until the man turned round. "Are you looking for anyone?"

"For Miss Rivière, sir. Some instructions are wanted about luncheon. But I was mistaken in supposing her to be in the belvedere. It is Mr. and Mrs. Pendleton who are there."

This, at least, was true. As Friary spoke, Edward and Irene Pendleton emerged from the building. They had much the air of cultivated tourists who have completed to their satisfaction the study of some minor antiquity.

"Since you are here," Appleby said to Friary, "may I ask you one or two questions? It's the convenient place, since they concern the belvedere."

"Irene and I must not barge in," Pendleton said. "We will make our way back to the house. Unless, of course, we can by any chance be of help."

"Then do stay for a moment." Appleby saw that the Pendletons were full of curiosity. "I think," he went on, turning to Friary, "that you passed the belvedere last night, on your way back from paying some call in the village?"

"That is correct." Friary's handsome features were not quite what they had been. There were dark rings under his eyes, and his expression was that of a man who knows that some ordeal lies ahead of him. Nevertheless he spoke steadily enough. "It was at precisely half-past nine, sir."

"But you didn't hear or see any sign of Mr. and Mrs. Martineau?"

"No."

"You are aware that, for some time past, they have been in the habit of coming up here occasionally in the evening?"

"Of course, sir. It was something very generally known."

"And on the previous night you were aware of them?"

"Yes."

"On that occasion, did you see them, or merely hear them talking?"

"It was only a matter of hearing, sir. If you will consider the position of this particular path in relation to the belvedere—"

"Quite so. You went by close to the building, but at a lower level, so that only its upper part would be visible. Were you actually able to distinguish what Mr. and Mrs. Martineau were saying?"

"A few words came to me, and then I had passed out of earshot. It would not have been proper to linger."

"Of course not. But, so far as what you did hear goes, it was a matter of entirely normal conversation?"

"Oh, most certainly. Mrs. Martineau, I believe, was saying something about the sunset, and its appearing to promise good weather on the following day. Yesterday, that would be."

"So it would. And that is the last time that you are aware of your late employers as having come up here?"

"No, sir. It is not."

"But you say that last night—"

"I am in no confusion, sir." Friary looked coldly at Appleby. Whether a trifle soft or not, the man wasn't without fight in him. "I don't think you will find that I have anything to retract."

"Well, that's very satisfactory. And now, just what is this later occasion you are speaking of?"

"It was yesterday afternoon, sir. The time was five o'clock precisely."

"You seem uncommonly fond of that sort of precision.

Just what—"

"Perhaps so, sir. But punctuality depends on an exact sense of time, and is important to one holding a position like mine."

"I'm sure that is so." Appleby was aware that a slight lilt of insolence had come into Friary's voice, but he paid no attention to it. "My question was going to be this. Just what were you doing up here at five o'clock?"

"Am I right in detecting a note of hostility in that question, sir?"

This time, the insolence had emerged with a bang. Edward Pendleton could be heard as making a disapproving noise.

"Everybody at Charne, Friary, must be prepared to accept stringent questioning." Appleby said this without irritation. "May I please have your answer?"

"Very well. Since the master and mistress took to using the belvedere in the way we are considering, I have made it my business to come up from time to time and see that things are in order. Domestically speaking, a garden house of this sort tends to be neither an indoor nor an outdoor responsibility. I have to see that the cleaning and so forth is not neglected. I trust that my explanation is in order, sir."

"Very well. And you say that Mr. and Mrs. Martineau were here at five o'clock yesterday afternoon?"

"At that hour precisely, sir—if the expression does not again offend you."

"You went in and spoke to them?"

"No. It was merely a matter of overhearing them, once more. I didn't think it proper to disturb them."

"No doubt you were right. And again it seemed to be a

matter of normal conversation?"

"Yes. It was exactly as on the previous night."

"Thank you, Friary. We needn't detain you further. But presently the Chief Constable wishes me to take a look at Mr. Martineau's office. I shall want you there then."

"As you say, sir." Friary produced his minimal bow. He was like a clergyman of the most Low-church persuasion, Appleby incongruously thought, civilly constrained to make a bob at the altar of a High-church colleague. And then he walked away. There was a moment's silence, before Edward Pendleton exploded in indignation.

"That fellow's a damned liar!" Pendleton said.

"It's only too likely." Appleby spoke grimly. "Quite apart from what's happened at Charne, Friary's in an uncommonly tight spot. In fact, he's booked for jail—and by now I think he knows it. He's got a girl in the village with child. And she's so impossibly young that he can't possibly get away with any plea of ignorance. He'll tell any lie." Appleby paused, and looked hard at Pendleton. "But, Edward, just what lie are you talking about?"

"His saying that he heard Charles and Grace up here at five o'clock yesterday afternoon. Irene, you can support me in this?"

"Most certainly. We all heard the stable clock." Irene Pendleton, although not without giving signs that the whole matter in hand was distasteful to her, spoke confidently and at once. "At five o'clock yesterday, Edward and I were talking to Grace in that beautifully warm corner of the walled garden. Friary is certainly lying."

"Not a doubt of it," Edward Pendleton said. "Nasty piece of work all round."

"Do you know, I find that rather interesting?"

Appleby said this so mildly that Judith looked at him swiftly. Not that she needed to look. For she knew instantly that the Commissioner of Police, careful not to trespass on a field that was none of his, politely helpful only if appealed to, anxious to get away from a false situation while the going was good—she knew that this John Appleby, whose façade might be described as having undergone a certain amount of erosion already, had now crumbled, tumbled, vanished in dust. . . .

"For just why," Appleby said, "should Friary tell precisely—the word's his, isn't it?—precisely *this* lie? We'll take a look inside the belvedere. And then we'll go down to Charles's office straightaway." He looked at his watch. "Morrison, you'll give me till midnight?"

"That's fair enough." The Chief Constable managed his casual note—but he was staring at this transformed person, all the same. "To the very stroke of the hour."

"Good," Appleby said. "Come along."

Chapter 19

THE DOUBLE DOORS of the belvedere, themselves elegantly curved to conform to the lines of the building, were wide open. The interior, although lit also from the small aperture above, somehow remained filled only with a subdued light. Once inside and looking outward, the effect was rather that of being in a miniature theatre, and of facing a proscenium arch beyond which was revealed a brightly lit rural scene. Alternatively one could close the doors and so find oneself in dim seclusion, with no other company than that of two sightless marble statues set in niches, and a vague proliferation of dolphins and other marine creatures on a somewhat cracked and damaged mosaic floor. There was provision for electric heating and lighting; there was a table together with a few comfortable chairs; there was even one of the ivory telephones. As fixtures there were some tall and elegant cupboards in a grey wood and of classical design. At one time these had no doubt served some purpose of refined living. When one opened them now—Appleby discovered —they disclosed merely a tumble of flower pots and similar oddments. The whole place, indeed, seemed to have been only casually reclaimed for occupation; near the back there was a barrow, a gardener's ladder, and a jumble of croquet boxes, golf bags, tennis nets and similar paraphernalia.

Here, it was to be supposed, the Martineaus had found their last contentment together. Perhaps because a consciousness of this hung in the air, one found oneself moving quietly, and not caring much to linger. The Pendletons, indeed, had gone off at once, so that the Applebys were again left alone with the Chief Constable. Three people were enough for one small and obvious experiment.

"You two can sit down," Appleby said. "More or less in the doorway, I'd say. When I give a whistle, you must contrive a couple of minutes' casual conversation. Would you be able to manage that?"

"I don't see why not." Colonel Morrison was once more rather forlornly humorous. "It oughtn't positively to tax our social resources."

"Then here goes," Appleby said, and walked back into the wood. When he returned five minutes later, it was to nod briskly. "Fair enough," he said. "Really no comment needed."

"You both heard our voices and could identify them?" Morrison asked.

"Definitely."

"And make out what we said?"

"A word or two. Judith said something about its being a fine evening, and of the sort that promised a fine day tomorrow."

"Yes. I thought I'd better go the whole hog." Judith

169

shivered suddenly. "Can we leave this place now?" she asked. "I somehow didn't like that experiment an awful lot."

"Then come along." Appleby turned to Morrison. "Ought the belvedere to be locked up?" he asked.

"I have a man keeping an eye on it. He made himself scarce when we turned up."

"Good. Now for the office."

"Those two kinds of motive," Judith said, as they made their way through the wood. "Greed and fear. You know, they may *both* apply to Bobby Angrave—and to Bobby Angrave alone."

"Making him an odds-on favourite, eh?" Morrison had showed a quick interest. "You know, I don't care for that young fellow, as I said. Too clever by half. Not that I'd let such feelings prejudice the matter in any way. But how do you mean, Lady Appleby?"

"There can be very little doubt that Bobby was his uncle's eventual heir. Probably there is a will of Charles's leaving Charne and a good deal else to his wife in the first place, for it was certainly wholly in Charles's power to dispose of. But ultimately he would have arranged that Bobby should inherit. Very well. That actually makes Bobby Angrave the owner of Charne at this moment, or at least as soon as various legal forms have been complied with. John, would that be right?"

"Almost certainly."

"But, until both Charles and Grace were dead, Bobby was only an heir on suffrance. He had no right in the property whatever."

"That must be so too."

"And so we have the motive of greed."

"But what about fear?" Morrison asked. "We've worked out the facts about Friary. Miss Page had exposed him to Mrs. Martineau. As soon as Mrs. Martineau passed on the story to her husband, Friary's number was up. But as Miss Page herself could be frightened into silence—"

"We've got all that." For the first time, Appleby spoke impatiently. "The point is that, for some reason, the *double* motive works with Bobby. And I think I know why."

"Quite suddenly, he was in a fix with his uncle and aunt," Judith said. "He said exactly that to me, when he more or less presented himself as top suspect. I felt he was simply trailing his coat. There's something perverse about the movement of Bobby's mind, even at the best of times. But perhaps it was all some kind of bluff. Anyway, it seems a fact that something was going to turn up that would wreck his chances, if he didn't act quickly."

"And, of course, we know what it was going to be." Appleby had turned to Morrison. "Would I be right in supposing you had quite a spot of trouble over drug-taking not so long ago—and actually among highly respectable county families?"

"Yes, indeed. Not surprised you've heard of it. A shocking thing. One boy driven potty. Another packed off to be a jackaroo in New South Wales or some such place. And a lot more mischief than that."

"Bobby Angrave admits to having been in on it. He spoke to me rather lightheartedly about it—but that was something he probably wouldn't have done unless there was trouble brewing. And that brings in Pendleton."

"Pendleton?" Morrison was blankly astonished. "Fellow's a bit too pleased with himself for my liking. But I can't believe he'd peddle—"

"No, no—it's not like that at all." Appleby was amused. "From Edward Pendleton we have to move on to one of the local doctors. He's the man who's been attending on Grace Martineau. His name is Fell."

"Fell? Yes, I've heard of him. Very well reputed, and all that."

"Well, Fell—although it appears to be going off at a tangent—is in the running as a suspect himself—under 'fear,' that is, not 'greed.'"

"My dear chap, haven't we got enough—"

"Oh, no." Appleby was suddenly cheerful. "One can't, you know, have too many suspects. The more you have, the likelier you are to nobble one of them."

It appeared to take Colonel Morrison a moment to gauge the frivolous character of this piece of logic. Having done so, he offered no comment.

"But we'll stick, for the moment, to Angrave. Charles Martineau suddenly becomes aware that his nephew has been taking drugs. It's impossible to see that as serious in itself. The boy quite clearly hasn't become any sort of addict, and he hasn't been involved in any open scandal. Charles Martineau is a man of the world, and a man of sense as well. So far, there's nothing that would persuade him to come down heavily on a lad who must still have been short of his majority during the time in question. On the other hand, Martineau, like his wife, is a person of high moral principle. If Bobby's conduct had something really vicious about it—if he had made money, say, by peddling the stuff to younger friends—that would finish him as certainly with his uncle, who liked him, as it would with his aunt, who did not. One can imagine a position, that's to say, in which Bobby would have to act swiftly or be disinherited."

They had now emerged from the wood, and Charne lay in front of them. Colonel Morrison halted for a moment to survey it. He might have been estimating just what it could be worth to a dislikeable young man who was too clever by half.

"That's a facer," he said. "If Angrave has got the wind up at this moment, I can't say that I'm surprised. But what could have brought the drug business home to him now? It's past history, more or less. At least, I hope it is."

"The answer to that is Dr. Fell. Or rather, it's a luckless encounter between Fell and our friend Pendleton. At the moment, I needn't go into details. But Fell has some scandal about drugs concealed in his past; Pendleton happens to know about it; and Pendleton thought it proper to give a very private warning to Martineau. It's clear that Martineau at once thought of that bad business of Bobby's local friends. He became alarmed, questioned Bobby, taxed Fell, probably made fresh inquiries at the other lads' homes. And here's our final point for the moment. Bobby may have been in sudden and unexpected danger. But so may Fell. Fell may actually have let people have drugs. Or, at the very least, he may have been so careless about them that—his record being in some way as it is—any further trouble would lead to his being struck off the Medical Register. But it was still only from the Martineaus that any such trouble could come."

"Edward Pendleton," Judith interrupted. "What

about him?"

"It's a point, certainly. Yet just consider. Edward is a very fair-minded man, and has the strongest possible sense of professional propriety. He considers that it would be wholly improper to breathe a word in public about Fell's past history, whatever it may have been. If Fell was ever actually charged with professional misconduct, he must either have been cleared, or penalized only in some minor way. Probably he turned G.P. simply because he realized it was imprudent to continue as an anaesthetist; no more than that. So all that Edward Pendleton does is to say this very confidential word to Charles. And then—"

"But wait a moment." Morrison had held up a hand to interrupt. "If Fell's past is not in any way really lurid, why should this admittedly awkward cropping up from it lead him towards desperate courses?"

"I've told you. The revelation of even a mild second involvement in irregularities over drugs might well be fatal to him. Moreover, he may have a present—or a recent past—that is *more* lurid than whatever trouble first checked his career. And now let me get back to Judith's question. Suppose there is this new threat—embodied solely in what the Martineaus may conceive it their duty to do. Suppose Grace Martineau then appears to die by a tragic accident, and her husband appears to take his own life in consequence. These misfortunes don't seem to have the slightest connection with Dr. Fell. They distress our friend Edward very much. And one very likely consequence is that Dr. Fell and his affairs never enter Edward's head again."

"It would be a most desperate gamble, all the same."

Colonel Morrison paused on the terrace. "Is there anybody else, Appleby, that you can work up a case against in this terrifying way?"

"Macaulay the gardener, perhaps. And, of course, his Aberdonian nephew. Or old Mr. and Mrs. Coombs at the lodge."

"No, no—my dear fellow. Seriously, more or less."

"Martine Rivière."

"Ah, the niece. But would she stand to inherit much?"

"At the moment, we just don't know. Certainly something. Perhaps she hasn't been altogether out of the running for a great deal. With one single changed circumstance, she would be a very good suspect indeed."

"And what's that?"

"A switching of the two deaths."

"Whatever do you mean by that?"

"Simply in point of time. It seems certain and established—doesn't it?—that Grace Martineau died before Charles. But suppose it had been the other way round. For a certain space of time, Grace would probably have been the owner of Charne and everything else. Like my wife, I can't imagine Charles Martineau as having made any other sort of will."

"But that's fantastic!" The Chief Constable seemed really upset. "To leave everything to a dying woman would simply be to invite red ruin in the way of death duties."

"Well, perhaps he didn't. Perhaps he bequeathed his wife only a life interest in Charne, with Bobby Angrave as the eventual proprietor. But he would quite certainly leave a great deal to his wife absolutely—and damn death duties. So my point, of course, is this. If Grace had survived Charles, it would be as the owner of substantial wealth, the eventual disposition of which could be determined in terms of an existing will. If Grace's will, say, left everything to Martine Rivière, who was her favourite, then Martine would get everything that had passed into Grace's estate at the time of her death. Roughly, it may be put this way: it was to Bobby Angrave's interest that Grace should die before Charles, and to Martine Rivière's interest that Charles should die before Grace. And Bobby won."

"Perhaps there was a hitch," Judith said.

"It's possible." Appleby laughed shortly. "But I doubt whether Martine is the sort that goes in for hitches."

Colonel Morrison had produced a silk handkerchief, and with this he mopped his brow. The day, it was true, was already turning warm; nevertheless there was a faint hint of the theatrical in his gesture.

"Now for Martineau's office," he said. "And I can only hope there's to be no hitch, my dear Appleby, in what you've pretty well promised me before midnight."

"It's unlikely. I can't say more than that."

"John is intolerable." Judith took her husband's arm. "Quite, quite intolerable. But he commonly brings these things off, all the same."

"I have faith in him," Morrison said. "When backed up by you." He hesitated. "By the way, perhaps I should mention . . . well . . . in Mr. Martineau's office,—"

"The body's still there?"

"Yes. The photographs have been taken, and the fingerprint work done, and so forth. But the matter of posture and so on is so crucial—"

"Yes, of course. And you won't want a crowd." Judith

was not in the least unwilling to be thus dismissed. "I think I see Martine in the loggia. I'll go and join her."

It was with evident relief that Morrison watched Judith move away.

"Face anything, I'm sure," he said. "But no reason to shove just this at her—eh? Don't mind telling you, it gave me a bit of a turn myself."

Chapter 20

BOBBY ANGRAVE stood in the hall. He was watching several plainclothes policemen packing miscellaneous equipment in boxes. There were two police cars and a van in front of the house, and several uniformed constables were also visible. Bobby turned away from this spectacle and advanced towards Morrison and Appleby. Although his manner made no parade of owning the place, he had in some way taken on an air of authority. This was partly evident in a careful courtesy.

"If it isn't holding you up," he said, "may I have a word with both of you?"

"Most certainly." Morrison's reply was brisk. "Anything you have to say, Mr. Angrave, is material. It will be considered carefully. Very carefully, indeed."

"There's nobody in the library." Bobby led the way there, let the others enter before him, and then shut the door. "I suppose," he asked politely, "that if one is proved to have committed suicide one is cast into prison at once?"

"Your question is meaningless, sir." Not surprisingly,

the Chief Constable's reception of this frivolity was stony. "The act of suicide is illegal, and the attempt is therefore illegal too. But, as you know perfectly well, at the present day it is seldom followed by the institution of criminal proceedings—unless there has been a suicide pact, or something of that sort."

"So it's very probable that your activities at Charne are not directed at finding a criminal?"

"They may well do so."

"That's just what I'm afraid of." Bobby Angrave produced this astonishing remark perfectly naturally. "Rather to your surprise, you may, in a sense, come upon a criminal. I wonder whether it's a good idea?"

"Mr. Angrave, it is hard for me to follow you. You cannot expect comment on the strength of such cryptic remarks."

"I'm only saying that it seems to me you might reasonably leave well alone."

"My dear Bobby"—Appleby thought he had better interrupt—"it isn't easy to describe as 'well' a state of affairs involving two unexplained unnatural deaths. It's the Chief Constable's concern to establish the truth, whether it leads to finding a criminal or not."

"And it seems to be your concern too, sir, since you've started mucking in." Bobby said this in a cheerful tone apparently designed to render the words tolerably inoffensive. "My point is, you know, that I don't believe you are going to find anybody to jug. I suspect that a stage will come when you both realize that. There won't be any justice to execute—and, if that's so, will it be all that sage and sensible to feel there's nevertheless a truth to vindicate? I know you both have a professional character, and all that. But I put it to you simply as between gentlemen."

"You seem to be suggesting conspiracy," Morrison said grimly.

"I suppose you can put it in that stuffy way, if you choose. But you know perfectly well what I mean." Bobby had walked to a window, and was surveying the terrace. "All those Black Marias, and big-bottomed blood-hounds straining at their leashes—"

"Mr. Angrave, I will not listen to offensive language about the men under my command."

"All right, Colonel, all right." Bobby allowed himself a flash of impertinence. "But you understand me perfectly well. Martineaus have been around this place for quite a long time. I'd have supposed the dossier could be closed without bringing in the Sunday reading of the folk. Or even the B.B.C. You know the kind of thing. A fellow with a disagreeable accent standing at the lodge gates and talking into the cameras about the dark mystery lying up the drive behind him."

There was a moment's silence. This was because Colonel Morrison had been reduced to speechlessness. He would have been less speechless, perhaps, if this outrageous old-school-tie stuff hadn't in fact touched some chord in him.

"I'd have supposed we could all be trusted," Bobby said. "If it came to the crunch, I mean." He turned round and looked straight at Appleby. "I appeal to you," he said. "My aunt drowned herself, because her few remaining weeks of life were not worth bearing. My uncle shot himself, because he had no wish to continue living."

"Bobby, are you stating what you believe to be the truth, or simply what you have a notion it's right and gentlemanlike to accept?"

"You know the answer to that one, perfectly well." Bobby turned to Morrison. "I'm right in believing," he asked, "that drowning is the method of suicide more commonly adopted by women than any other?"

"No, you are not."

"But among my Aunt Grace's age group it is true?"

"Yes—in the sense that drowning headed the statistics until not so very long ago."

"Men, on the other hand, don't reject methods involving bloodshed and disfigurement?"

"That is true. Mr. Angrave, you appear curiously in command of the technicalities of this subject."

"I've been reading the *Encyclopaedia Britannica*—my uncle's copy, which is rather an old one. So you must forgive me if I'm a little out of date. My point is that everything has happened—"

"By the book?" Appleby asked.

"You can put it that way. I was going to say, simply, in a perfectly natural manner." Bobby paused, and eyed the two elderly men before him. He appeared to determine that he had effected nothing. "You must go ahead," he said abruptly. "You must go ahead, and unearth your pain and scandal. I don't want to exaggerate, you know. It won't prove all that awful."

"We shall certainly go ahead." Morrison spoke stiffly. "At the moment, and for a start, we are going into your uncle's office. I understand that Sir John would like to see the butler, Friary, there. May I ask you to be so very kind as to send him to us?"

"Very well. And, no doubt, you must follow your own lights. I go on record as thinking it a pity. That's all."

Bobby Angrave turned and left the room. Morrison

watched him go in silence, and then turned to Appleby.

"I can't make that young man out at all. What was he after? Have you any idea?"

"Well, yes—I think I have. There may come a point at which we have a lurking feeling he was right."

"Good God, Appleby! You don't mean you think we should drop the thing, and let the coroner have his jury bring in their two harmless verdicts?"

"Far from it. And now we'll view Charles Martineau's body."

"One can see why he would come straight in here," Appleby said, when the body had been covered up again. "It would be the natural place from which to telephone for help."

"Martineau did just that. He called Fell."

"And Fell was at home?"

"No, but he got back from some call or other fifteen minutes later."

"I suppose Fell could walk straight into the house if he wanted to?"

"I'm sure he could. And it's a habit busy doctors have."

"So while Martineau was in the act of telephoning for Fell, Fell could have walked in here and killed him?"

"Not a doubt of it." Colonel Morrison produced his silk handkerchief again. "But I'm not sure he would know about the gun. And I think the gun would have had to be secured beforehand. It was kept, loaded, in the top drawer of that desk."

"Locked up there?"

"Unlocked. It's amazing what people will do. Martineau doesn't even appear to have troubled me for a licence for the damned thing." Morrison paused broodingly. "It doesn't seem to me likely that Fell would know about it."

"I rather agree. But any member of the household might. Friary, for example, is a type who would poke about in drawers. And either of the young people might know."

"Yes—but not Mrs. Gillingham. Not that that's relevant." Morrison was faintly ironical. "She's supposed only to have eliminated Martineau's wife, and not Martineau himself as well. . . . Come in." There had been a knock at the door. Friary entered. And Appleby tackled him at once.

"Friary, I suppose you keep a general eye on this room?"

"Certainly, sir. I have regarded its oversight as a regular part of my duties." It couldn't be said that Friary's nervous tone was improving; indeed, he had now taken to glancing apprehensively about him. But there was still something faintly contemptuous in his bearing. It emerged, Appleby reflected, in his manner of speech. Friary talked like a stage butler, one had to suppose, because he was inwardly unreconciled to being a real one.

"Very well. Will you be good enough to tell me whether you notice anything unusual about the room now?"

"The presence of Mr. Martineau's body might be so described, sir."

This produced an impatient exclamation from Colonel Morrison, as well it might. But Appleby was unmoved.

"That, of course, is true. But look about you carefully.

Are you aware of anything missing, or anything disarranged?"

Friary obeyed this instruction. He even made a circuit of the small room, giving the dead man under his sheet a wide berth.

"I am not conscious of anything out of the way, sir."

"Thank you. But would you mind looking at the writing table beside the fireplace? It has, I think, fairly recently had a new leather top?"

"That is so."

"Look at the surface. Do you see four very slight circular depressions, which form a square, and are set about a foot apart?"

"I believe I can just distinguish what you refer to, sir."

"Of course you can." Appleby's tone was suddenly sharp. "What is it that commonly stands there, and isn't there now?"

"I am afraid I cannot say." Friary, who had been scrutinizing the leather surface of the table with exaggerated care, looked up with a wooden face. "Possibly Mr. Martineau's typewriter."

"That is on the desk, and its dimensions are quite different. I am afraid I must press you about this. It can't, you know, really be beyond your recollection."

There was a moment's silence. It would have been hard to tell whether Friary was uneasy before the particular point at issue, or whether he was simply ceasing to stand up well to the total situation. He licked his lips.

"I beg your pardon, sir. You are quite right. It has come back to me. What usually stands there is Mr. Martineau's tape recorder."

"A tape recorder?" Morrison, who had been staring

gloomily out of the window, turned round and stared at Appleby instead.

"I see," Appleby said. "And where is this tape recorder now?"

"Undergoing repair, I believe, sir. Mr. Martineau mentioned to me a week or two ago that he had taken it into town for that purpose. Presumably he had not picked it up again. And it has certainly not been delivered at Charne."

"Do you happen to know just where he took it?"

"Yes, sir. He was specific about it. Curtis and Redpath, in High Street."

"Thank you. We needn't detain you longer now."

Morrison waited until the door had closed behind Friary.

"I suppose it's nonsense," he said. "But—do you know?—I never hear of a tape recorder without remembering some mystery story or other. By one of those dashed clever women who concoct such things. Frightfully good. Only, of course, I don't remember how it was brought in. . . . Sorry." Morrison had become aware that Appleby was at the telephone.

The call took only a couple of minutes.

"Well," Appleby said, as he put down the receiver, "—you heard *that*. Just what do you make of it?"

"You're sure you were actually speaking to Curtis and Whatever?"

"Of course I am."

"Martineau must have changed his mind. Taken the thing somewhere else."

"It's a possibility, of course. But it doesn't quite fit with what the fellow in the shop said. Martineau always took his electrical gadgets of all sorts there. He'd done so for years."

"In that case our friend Friary is a damned liar—which is something that I take it we're pretty sure of already. Pinched the thing himself, I suppose. But what would he have done that for?"

"Curtis and Redpath sold it to Martineau. You heard me ask about that. They say that, although not bulky, it's a very high-class instrument. You may laugh at your dashed clever women, Morrison. But there's almost no limit to the tricks that can be played with such a thing."

"And here is Friary telling lies about it."

"Telling one more lie—and one more lie very easy to detect, at that."

"My dear Appleby—just what are you getting at?"

"Friary mayn't have lied to us." Appleby spoke slowly. "Charles Martineau may have lied to Friary."

Chapter 21

JUDITH HAD WANDERED into the wood again. Not far from the belvedere—when she could see, indeed, the flat-capped figure of the constable now guarding it—she ran into Dr. Fell. It was a mildly surprising encounter, and Fell himself appeared almost disconcerted. He came to a halt, and looked at Judith uncertainly.

"Good morning, Dr. Fell. Are you going down to the house?"

"I am going wherever I can find the police, Lady Appleby. If possible, the Chief Constable himself."

"He is there, and so is my husband. They are probably still in Mr. Martineau's office."

"Thank you." Fell made as if to move on again, and then hesitated. "It's a revolting business," he said. "But action I suppose there must be."

"The Martineaus' death, you mean?"

"No. That is very sad, of course. I gather it is now thought to be suspicious and sinister, into the bargain. It may well be so. But it wasn't what I was thinking of. Ugly things are coming to light all over the place, are they not? In a matter of this sort, one scandal shakes up another."

"No doubt." Judith found this vague and uneasy remark curious. "The suggestion of some sort of drug ring, for example."

"You know about that?" Fell, who had to walk on beside Judith, came to a halt. "It's certainly in the picture."

"I know about it—and that Bobby Angrave felt it was going to make life awkward for him."

"And that I feel the same?" Fell looked at Judith with a faint smile. "You are a very direct person, Lady Appleby."

"What's the good of not being?"

"What, indeed. Well, I suspect it is true that Angrave had been a good deal more than silly. Something of the sort is sure to emerge, and it may as well be stated now. . . . Is that a policeman by the belvedere?"

"Yes. Was it there you were expecting to find Colonel Morrison? You were on the path to it, really."

"It was in my head." Fell produced this in his sudden vague manner. "Shall we go on there now? I value having a word with you."

"Very well." Judith walked on. "But you began by saying that something is a revolting business."

"The Martineaus' butler and this village child your husband called me in to see. She's prepared to name Friary as responsible, and there is evidence that her parents can give as well. So it will come into court. I ought to be hardened to such things, but I don't seem to be."

"Dr. Fell, do you think that, as the matter stood yesterday, it would have been rational in Friary to suppose that if the Martineaus were out of the way he would have a chance of not being prosecuted?"

"Good heavens!" Fell looked really startled. "It's possible, I suppose. But I didn't know there was a suspicion of just that sort. For that matter, I doubt whether the fellow Friary would have the guts for it. No—I think I'm a better suspect myself."

"I find that a strange thing for anyone actually to say."

"I had a meeting, you know, or what might be called a confrontation, with Martineau and his nephew. Over the drugs. Its issue was unsatisfactory, from my point of view."

"And from Bobby's?"

"Oh, certainly. Martineau penetrated to the fact that Bobby had actually been peddling the stuff, and he remained unconvinced that I wasn't myself in some way involved."

"Were you?" Judith had decided that this curious conversation had better be gone through with.

"For what the denial is worth, Lady Appleby, quite definitely not. But—for reasons into which I needn't enter—if some large scandal blew up in these parts, I mightn't get a fair spin."

"We know about that. So really, you feel, you and Bobby Angrave had substantial reason to conspire together to silence the Martineaus?"

"I hadn't thought of just that. But I see what you mean. If the Martineaus *were* both murdered, and if the circumstances were to prove such that there must have been two people on the job, then young Angrave and I would—to put it mildly—be well in the picture." Fell, who had produced this quite unemotionally, walked for a moment in silence. "But here is the belvedere," he said.

"Do you know, I've never had a look inside? Would that constable let us in?"

"I think he might. He knows me now. We'll have a try."

The constable made no objection. He contented himself with accompanying his visitors into the interior of the little building.

"Colonel Morrison and my husband have already had a good hunt through the place," Judith said. "We came in together earlier this morning."

"Did you discover anything material?"

"Did I? I'm afraid not—although I always have a feeling there ought to be something a woman's eye can contribute." Judith looked around her. "For example, it's a little dusty, wouldn't you say? Friary claims to see that it is cleaned, and so forth. But the floor would certainly do with a mop. Look how—" Judith broke off. "Dr. Fell, will you move that gardener's ladder so that it stands just *there*? With its two feet just on these marks, I mean."

Fell did as he was told. The constable made an uneasy noise. Then, presumably recalling the exalted station of this lady's husband, he fell silent again.

"You see what I mean?" Judith pointed. "It's the ladder that has been drawn over the floor, and left these tracks."

"It looks," Fell said, "as if somebody had wanted to climb to the top of those cupboards."

"You're quite right. And there might be anything up there, behind those rather elaborate cornices—if that's what they should be called. I think I'll go up and see." Judith looked at the cupboards more carefully. "What's that cord," she asked, "running up the side of the far one?"

"It's an electric wire, my lady." The constable said this, after examination. "The telephone, perhaps. But no—it isn't that." He had followed the wire downward, and was now moving a croquet box away from the skirting board. "It's simply plugged into a socket down here. It may run to a lamp, I'd say, or it might be a small radiator, that somebody has stored up there."

"Well, we'll see." Judith was already climbing. "Dr. Fell, just steady it, will you? I don't want to make a fool of myself."

At this moment the constable came to a somewhat apprehensive attention. Colonel Morrison and Appleby had entered the belvedere. Judith, who had gained the position she wanted, turned round and looked down at them.

"John," she said, "I've found something up here. You'll never guess what."

"I certainly shall," Appleby said. "It's a tape recorder. Don't touch it."

It was half an hour before the tape recorder was brought down from its place of concealment. It had to be photographed and tested for fingerprints first. At length it stood on a rustic table in front of Appleby.

"We'll run it back for a minute, for a start," Appleby said, "and then see what it offers us." He turned a couple of switches on the machine. Nothing happened. "Constable," he said, "switch it on down there by the skirting board, will you?"

"It's switched on already, sir."

"Then there's something wrong with it. And I doubt whether that makes sense." Appleby paused, frowning. "What have you got down there?"

"A plug with its own fuse, sir. It's on a modern thirteen-amp circuit."

"Try that reading lamp in the corner."

"Yes, sir. . . . It works, all right."

"Find a screwdriver, or whatever is needed, and change those plugs round."

"Very good, sir."

This operation took five minutes. They were five minutes which added considerably to the tension of the proceedings. Fell, who had remained in the belvedere, paced it moodily. Colonel Morrison eyed him with disfavour, and would plainly have been pleased to order him out. Martine Rivière, who had appeared again, was reduced to sitting close to Judith, nervously twisting a handkerchief.

"What's it about?" Martine almost whispered. "What does Sir John expect?"

"I don't know. I only know that *he* knows—and that it's important."

"All in order, sir." The constable stood up. "You can try again."

Appleby once more moved the switches. A tiny hum came at once from the machine, followed by the whir of the tape being fed back.

"That's all it was," Appleby said. "The fuse had blown. Careless. Odd."

"What's that, Appleby?" Morrison had moved forward. But Appleby raised an arresting finger; stopped the tape; set it moving again in the opposite direction.

And at once they were all listening to voices. They were listening to the voices of Charles and Grace Martineau.

The dialogue continued only for seconds. Appleby had switched off—with a decisive snap, and almost as if closing down upon premature disclosure.

"There's a little more to do," he said. "Not much. We'll meet—everybody will meet—in half an hour's time in the music room." He smiled rather grimly. "It's the appropriate place."

"For somebody to be facing the music, eh?" Colonel Morrison offered this suggestion uncertainly.

"That, perhaps. And, of course, it's a place dedicated to the educated ear."

"To the *what*, my dear fellow?"

"And moreover"—Appleby was unheeding—"it's presided over by Christopher Sly."

Chapter 22

"You may notice," Appleby said half an hour later, "that there is one person missing. Let me begin with that."

"Someone missing?" Edward Pendleton looked round the music room. "We're all here, as far as I can see."

"It depends what you mean by 'we,' Edward. Friary is missing."

"Oh, I see." Pendleton was disconcerted. "Well, go ahead."

"Friary is missing because he is in police custody. In what I have to say I shall have to speak for him, if it may be put like that."

"Friary will certainly need speaking for." Bobby Angrave said this. "We're nearly all in a mess. But I believe Friary is the only person who has been caught out in a pack of lies."

"He has been very notably caught out, it may be maintained, in two. And uncommonly interesting lies they are." Appleby paused to look round the company. As if distrustful of each other, they were dispersed in a wide circle round the music room. Although there were ten people, all told, they gave little impression of a crowd in the large and rather encumbered place. Behind them Holman Hunt's more numerous Shakespearian gathering continued its musical activities unconcerned. The tape recorder, again disposed in front of Appleby, might have been waiting to record the ghostly concert.

"So Friary will be available as required," Appleby went on. "Actually, there are two other people who are rather vital to our inquiry, but whom I haven't asked to attend. I can speak for them too. They are Mr. Macaulay, our late host's head gardener, and his nephew—a lad called Neil. As you know, it was they who found Grace Martineau's body. But they have another interest for us as well."

"Do you mean," Martine Rivière asked, "that they are suspects too?"

"And brought in," Bobby Angrave added, "to add a final touch of the grotesque to this farcical riot of suspicions?"

The aggressive question produced a moment's silence. Bobby and Martine were now the single exception to the scattered disposition of the company, for Martine had crossed the room and sat down close by her cousin. The effect was of a suddenly consolidated alliance. They might have been preparing to fight something—and fight it every inch of the way.

"Macaulay and his nephew are in no sense suspects." Appleby was unperturbed. "They merely have evidence to give. What weight is to be accorded to that evidence it may eventually be for a judge and jury to decide. Equally, it may not. You will find that you have a very open question before you. That's the first thing to get clear."

"You mean, Sir John, that there may in fact have been no crime?" It was Mrs. Gillingham who asked this. "That has always been the likeliest supposition, to my mind."

"It is not necessarily what I am thinking of. But let me begin, if the Chief Constable will allow me, with a plain fact. It is the existence of this machine, which you see in front of me. There is no question but that it belonged to Charles Martineau. He used it for business purposes—and also, as many people do, for recording music from time to time. It was found in the belvedere this morning."

"In the belvedere?" Edward Pendleton repeated. "I'm blessed if I saw it."

"The machine was stowed in an invisible position on top of a cupboard. It was plugged in, however, and so ready either to record or play back. Except for one fact. A fuse—the kind that is located in the actual plug—was defective. When we replaced this, the machine worked. But what it produced was neither business correspondence nor music. It was a conversation between the Martineaus."

"How very peculiar!" Irene Pendleton had for some reason taken it into her head to contribute to the discussion at this point. "Do you think, John, that Charles and Grace played some sort of game with it? Usually, they played piquet."

"It is possible, no doubt."

"May I say that I think this intolerable?" Bobby had returned to the attack. "There is an obvious explanation, and it is a very painful one. My uncle wanted to preserve some record of my aunt's conversation, since he knew that her death was not far off. And he secured it by concealing the machine in the belvedere, where they were in the habit of going to talk. He wouldn't want her to know what he was doing, I imagine. It is outrageous that you should be charging him with some obscure criminal intention."

"You may be right." Appleby looked at Bobby gravely. "And here I come to Macaulay and his nephew. What they have to say powerfully supports your interpretation. If your uncle was indeed concerned to conceal the machine, it would appear to have been from your aunt only. About a week ago, they both recall him as walking through the wood with it—and perfectly openly. There can be no mistake about this. They have identified the tape recorder without hesitation."

"And then the fingerprints," Colonel Morrison said.

"Ah, yes—the fingerprints." Appleby nodded. "The machine, when discovered, showed Martineau's fingerprints, and no others. But I still confess to a little doubt." Appleby said this very mildly. "This, if it happened, was a kind of sacred thing. I'm willing to agree with Mr. Angrave that it is most distressing that we should have to discuss it. Yet discuss it we must. I have to ask myself whether Charles Martineau would, in fact, think to obtain this record covertly. Knowing him, and knowing his relations with his wife, I feel it to be a large question. Then again—although it's quite another thing—I have to confess to a further doubt. I'm a little worried, if the truth be told, about that blown fuse. You see, the machine is in no way defective. That the fuse should simply have gone is, of course, technically possible. But it's such an unlikely thing to happen, you know, that one is bound to pause on it. And I'd emphasize this. In fact, quite frankly, I find it the most intractable element in the whole affair."

Dr. Fell, who had sat silent and brooding hitherto, suddenly stirred on his chair. He looked round the music room, and his glance rested on Diana Page.

"About Angrave's suggestion," he said, "it happens that I have something to say. I think Miss Page knows what I mean, and will support my doubtless suspect testimony." Fell frowned, as if regretting this gratuitous irony. "About a week ago—"

Fell broke off. He did so because Diana had burst into tears. It was a moment before he could resume.

"Miss Page and I were talking with Charles Martineau in a desultory way. He was teasing Miss Page a little—I think it may be put like that—about some sort of popular music. Is that not right?"

Diana nodded dumbly. She had controlled her sobbing.

"Then we spoke of the recording of music—and also of poetry. I think I mentioned having heard the voice of Tennyson on an old gramophone record. Miss Page—"

"Let me tell." Diana looked up and took a deep breath. Her tear-stained face held its not unfamiliar expression of mingled defiance and misery. "I'm so damned stupid! Of course I didn't mean to hurt him. But I said we could now all have such records—in families, and that sort of thing. So that we'd be able—" Diana failed to continue. She was weeping again.

Judith Appleby crossed the room, and sat down beside her.

"Diana," she said, "it wasn't really stupid, at all. And

now Dr. Fell can go on."

"There's little more to tell. It's true that, as a result of the turn our talk had taken, this idea seemed to be before us: that Charles Martineau—or merely one in his situation, say—might have that sort of record, just as he might have a portrait, or photographs in an album. The significant point is Martineau's reaction. For some reason he was horrified. He made it clear that the idea was repugnant to him. I don't suppose that Miss Page and I are doing more than recording an odd coincidence. But there it is."

"I don't think it is at all surprising." Martine Rivière had turned pale, but she made this interruption unemotionally. "Had my uncle casually possessed such a thing, he might have prized it. But I can see him recoiling from the notion of deliberately securing such a memorial at . . . at a late hour."

"I agree," Bobby Angrave said. "My explanation was a bad one." He hesitated. "But I have a queer feeling that Uncle Charles's conversation with Dr. Fell and Diana about recordings may have . . . well, put ideas in his head. Is there any sense in that? I suppose not."

"On the contrary, it may well be true." Appleby was looking across the room at his friend Christopher Sly. "And it mayn't be easy to tell just where the process stopped. For the moment, however, let me come back to Friary."

"And to his lies?" Bobby asked.

"Yes—but we must consider whether they were lies. The first relates to this tape recorder. According to Friary, Charles Martineau said he had taken it away to be repaired. This was not so. But why should Friary make

199

up such a story? Well, one can imagine motives—such as his having himself taken the machine for some evil design of his own. Had he done that, however, he would scarcely have told so readily detectable a lie. I had only to check on his story, and it would be exposed. It seems more likely that the lie—or prevarication—was Martineau's own, and Friary's statement quite truthful. Martineau proposed to use the machine in a way that he didn't care that Friary should know of—and therefore said something other than the truth about it. Remember, on the other hand, that he wasn't being consistently secretive. Macaulay and Neil saw him with the thing quite openly. And now take Friary's other seemingly motiveless lie. It too was vulnerable to exposure—if, once more, it was a lie, or if he knew that it was."

"About hearing his employers?" the Chief Constable asked.

"Exactly. Friary maintains that he heard the Martineaus talking together in the belvedere on the evening of the day before yesterday. Yesterday, the day of their deaths, he did *not* hear them at the same hour—the hour of his regular return from the village. But he *did* hear them, he says, much earlier—when he went up to the belvedere at five o'clock with the idea of seeing that everything was in order. According to Mr. and Mrs. Pendleton, however, this was impossible. They were themselves talking to Grace Martineau at that hour in quite another part of the grounds. Unless, once more, Friary is making up a story for reasons we haven't got at—and I really rule that out—there is only one explanation. It lies in this." Appleby tapped the tape recorder in front of him. "What Friary heard yesterday afternoon was a recorded conversation. Charles Martineau may have been in the belvedere; Grace Martineau cannot have been. So what are we to make of that?" Appleby paused. "I can think of only one reasonable explanation. Friary went to the belvedere on this occasion more or less by chance. His presence cannot have been reckoned on. So the performance, if we may call it that"—Appleby tapped the machine again—"was not designed for his benefit. It can scarcely have been for anyone's benefit. In fact it was a rehearsal— and being carried out in what was thought of as privacy."

"A rehearsal?" Colonel Morrison had produced his silk handkerchief; he was plainly bewildered. "A rehearsal for what? There's no record of this phoney conversation's ever being heard again."

"You have to remember the blown fuse," Appleby said.

In the baffled pause that followed, it was to be seen that Bobby Angrave had risen to his feet.

"I have protested about this," he said, "and I protest again now. I have no power to stop you from going on to whatever wretched conclusion you please. But I think I can forbid its happening in this house. You are hounding somebody you can't bring to justice—and you shan't do it here. Martine, you agree?"

"I don't think I do. I thought I did, but now I don't. I'm sorry, Bobby. But I think it must go on."

"It will go on, anyway." Bobby flung himself back in his chair. "But why not in their beastly police station, or coroner's court? However, have it your own way."

"Then I shall continue." Appleby looked at the young man seriously. "But I agree that we have arrived at a point at which it is possible to sympathize with the feeling you express. And now"—and Appleby looked round the company—"what is the first question we have to ask?"

For a moment it appeared that Appleby's own question was to be taken as rhetorical, and nobody spoke. When he remained silent, however, Pendleton provided a reply.

"The first question we have to ask is clear enough. I don't like it—but there it is in front of us. Just why should Charles have made such a recording, and just why should he have rehearsed it, as you term it, in the way he did?"

"Thank you." Appleby nodded sombrely. "Ask oneself that, and there is only one reply. Charles Martineau killed his wife."

Chapter 23

IT WAS INTO a stricken silence that Appleby next spoke. "Listen, please," he said—and set going the tape recorder. It was three or four minutes before he switched it off. "A very ordinary conversation, wouldn't you say? It even has a little of what Charles and Grace confessed to us: that they liked a mild gossip about their guests. But what are we to suppose? We are to suppose that Charles certainly recorded it because he knew his wife would die soon. But it was with a very different purpose from the simple commemorative one which Mr. Angrave was suggesting to us. Briefly, he was no longer able to bear the spectacle of her suffering, and he decided that he must kill her. A mercy killing is what the newspapers call it.

"But he didn't intend that this miserable thing should ever be known. He determined that Grace should meet the appearance of accidental death—death by drowning —and that he himself, for greater security, should own an alibi. So he recorded this talk—in the belvedere, no doubt. Yesterday afternoon—overheard by Friary, as it happened—he tested it out there. And then he was ready.

"Yesterday evening he and Grace made their little expedition together. On the way to the belvedere he drowned her in the pond. It was just like that." Appleby was silent for a moment. "And what then? His plan depended on the celebrated punctuality of Friary. He went on to the belvedere, and waited for Friary to pass. As soon as Friary approached, Martineau was going to switch on the tape recorder. Then, when he was sure that Friary had heard it, he was going to switch it off, *and at once join Friary*. He was going to see to it that Friary didn't take a path past the pond, *and he was going to remain within sight of one person or another until his wife's body had been found*. But, as it happened, his plan didn't work."

Diana Page was weeping again, but this time nobody attended to her. Mrs. Gillingham's sense of the importance of the forms didn't prevent her from looking like a woman who knows that she is in the presence of guilt and misery. Bobby Angrave and Martine Rivière had scarcely taken their eyes off each other since Appleby began his recital. But now Bobby looked across the room.

"What do you mean," he asked, "by saying that the plan didn't work?"

"Remember the extraordinary mischance of the fuse. The tape recorder failed to function, and Friary, as a consequence, walked past a belvedere from which there came nothing but silence. We may imagine that by this time Charles Martineau knew that he had behaved like a madman, and we may take a guess that he simply wandered about. When young Neil came with the news of Mrs. Martineau's death, some instinct of self-preservation made him—for a few futile minutes—play a part. He went into his office and summoned Dr. Fell. Then he took out that revolver and killed himself. Perhaps he had meant to do that all along."

There was a deep silence. Diana, becoming aware of the sound of her own sobs, was frightened into silence too.

"All that," Appleby said, "is what we are asked to suppose."

"You mean it isn't the truth?" Martine demanded.

"Of course not. Charles could not conceivably have thrust his wife into a pond and drowned her. Such a notion is nothing but a morbid fantasy. Yet a good deal has been built upon it."

"You mean that nothing of all this was ever so much as in my uncle's head?"

"Virtually that, Martine, I am glad to say. And yet it began with your uncle—and not wholly without a touch of the fantastic. It began, too, with this machine. Indeed, I am now going to play you another tape." Appleby busied himself with the tape recorder. "This one didn't have to be homemade. It can be obtained from some educational supplier or other. It's wonderful what children are taught nowadays. This tape, by the way, wasn't in the belvedere. It was found by some of Colonel Morrison's men in a place where I told them to hunt for it. It was in its cardboard box, which has proved useful for fingerprints. It would never have occurred to me to hunt for it, incidentally, but for a fellow called Christopher Sly."

"Christopher Sly?" Martine repeated.

"A tinker. I'll explain in a moment. Now listen, please." The tape recorder once more gave its little preliminary hum. And then, with an effect which might have startled the ears even of Holman Hunt's shadows on the walls, the music room at Charne was overflowing with the song of a nightingale.

Chapter 24

"Wilt thou have music? hark! Apollo plays,
And twenty caged nightingales do sing."

Appleby had switched off before offering his hearers
this quotation. The people in the music room were silent
for a time—just as they might have been had they been
gathered in the loggia at dusk, and the same strains been
filling the air.

"That's what they say to poor Sly in the play," Appleby said. "And I knew, quite early on, that Sly had
something to say to *me*. He sent me, as it were, a tiny signal. The signal was 'nightingale.' No more than that. In a
sense, it was in fact to prove to be a caged nightingale."
Appleby's hand was on the tape recorder still. He shook
his head, as if not well satisfied with himself. "This momentary signal ought to have linked itself—or *I* ought to
have linked it—with another which I'd received already.
You remember our talk about nightingales and poetry? I
knew there was *something* just catching at my mind at
that time. But I didn't get it."

"I don't think we know what you're talking about," Bobby Angrave said.

"I rather believe that somebody knows. Essentially, I'm talking about the possession of a good ear—or just an educated ear—and a precise auditory memory. I happen to have these. If Martine went to the piano now, and played to us a piece I'd heard her play yesterday, her two performances would both be available to me for critical comparison—supposing I were a critic, which I'm not."

"This is utter rot, to my mind." Bobby said this with cold contempt. "But I suppose you must go on—and on and on."

"I shall certainly go on, and I ask everybody to be patient. I am not the only person here with the kind of memory I speak of. Diana has it—and so has somebody else. Only Diana's memory is a little weak elsewhere. It's not very good at literary history."

"What do you mean?" Diana Page was staring at Appleby, bewildered and prepared once more to be terrified.

"Nothing alarming, Diana. But you did think that 'He sings each song twice over' was said by Browning about the nightingale. And when Bobby made fun of you, do you remember what you replied? It was: *This one has sung tonight exactly as he sang last night.* Well, it was literally true. Subconsciously, I was myself aware of the fact—for of course I too had heard the song on the previous night. And that was my first signal, you see."

"But it's meaningless!" Martine, pale and round-eyed, burst out with this. "Why should anyone—" She broke off, and her eyes filled with tears. "You mean that Uncle Charles made the nightingale sing in order to give pleasure to Aunt Grace?"

"Yes. He couldn't bring back the kingfishers, but he could bring back—or appear to bring back—the voice of the nightingale. It was his only deception, and a sufficiently strange one. But it brought another, and very different, deception into being. A third person, besides Diana and myself, got that tiny signal—and made much more of it. Went straight off to investigate, in fact. The recorded conversation between Charles and Grace owes its existence to that. And here let me tell you of something that Friary said. Describing that conversation as he heard it at five o'clock yesterday afternoon, he said it was *exactly as on the previous night*. His words almost echo Diana's on the nightingale's song."

"Do you mean," Martine asked, "that Friary heard a merely recorded conversation twice? Or that on the first occasion he heard a real conversation, and on the second a recording of it?"

"The latter. Which means that when the real conversation was taking place, the recording of it was being made."

"But that takes us back, doesn't it, to what Bobby was suggesting? If Uncle Charles made this recording on his machine—"

"Your uncle didn't make it, Diana. It was made by somebody else, on another machine, and without either your uncle or your aunt being aware of the fact. And now, I think, we have got to the end of the road."

There was silence for a time, and then Bobby Angrave spoke. It was with the air of casual inconsequence which he sometimes affected.

"You know, it's odd about the nightingale." Bobby

209

lounged to his feet. "I don't say its song isn't overrated. Still, it's something very pleasant to hear. So why should the Greeks have made it the centre of one of their most beastly old myths? Pandion and Tereus, you know, Procne and Philomela. How loathsome! And yet I've put in nearly all my young years studying the stuff. In future I shall study something quite different. Will you excuse me for a moment, by the way?" He had turned to Appleby.

"Yes," Appleby said. He looked at the young man steadily. "Of course."

Without haste, Bobby walked to the door and opened it. "But just what," he said, turning round for a moment, "shall I study, instead of all that Greek and Latin? A long silence, perhaps."

He was gone. It was a second before Colonel Morrison, with a quick glance of astounded indignation at Appleby, rose and dashed for the door too. But the music room was too impeded for rapid movement. Before he could gain his goal, there was a shout and the sound of running feet from outside—as if some of his own men, perhaps, had taken alarm. Then, within what seemed seconds, a loud report was heard from somewhere across the hall.

"We shall meet again later," Appleby said presently. "For the moment, I think it is by the library that everybody should go out. And the gun room, perhaps, is a place to avoid."

"Good God, John!" Edward Pendleton had got to his feet, pale and shaken. "You mean—"

"I have no doubt that Bobby is dead. He said, I remember, that at the end of this affair there would be no-

210

body to bring to justice. That was because he had so cunningly cast his uncle in the role of the criminal, and his uncle—he had managed to suggest—had killed himself. But now it is literally true. Bobby was the murderer. He has chosen to escape the dock."

Appleby rose, grim and strained, and walked over to his wife.

Chapter 25

"DIDN'T BOBBY LOSE his nerve?" Judith asked. The Applebys were driving back to London. "Could it have been brought home to him?"

"Certainly it could. And he knew it as soon as I uttered the words *on another machine.*"

"I don't follow that."

"It's simple enough. You remember him driving off in the morning in his car, and talking some nonsense about visiting the good poor? It was his first move towards the murders. The night before, and just before I had my long talk with him in the garden, he had discovered Charles's tape recorder in the belvedere, and tumbled to the secret of the nightingale. His mind—I can now see—was in a whirl of excitement. He talked of the insane things that love, passion, even affection can make a man do. He said he *knew.* And so he did. He had been suddenly confronted by the pathos of Charles Martineau's last gift to his wife. He talked of other things as well: euthanasia, murder, Lord knows what. But I believe his mind was working all the time. And, early in the formation of his plan, he must have seen one thing clearly. Charles's tape recorder, if Charles's fingerprints were to be found undisturbed on it, must be handled very carefully. He just couldn't risk using it for *his* proposed covert recording. Hence his hurrying off, and buying a small instrument, which could easily be concealed. It was very rash, since it meant that, if he came under suspicion, his purchase would almost certainly be discovered. Only he didn't mean to come under suspicion. It was his uncle—his uncle whom he had murdered—who was to come under suspicion. Suspicion of killing Grace, whom Bobby had in fact murdered too."

"Would there have been any other proof?"

"Bobby's own fingerprints were on the box that we found the recording of the nightingale in. And it was hidden in his room."

"Then he did have to handle Charles's recorder to the extent of removing the nightingale tape and substituting the one he had secured of his uncle and aunt talking?"

"Of course."

"But why on earth didn't he then destroy the nightingale tape?"

"Conceit. It was to be a secret trophy. Do you know—I believe that if we hadn't gone to Charne, all this might never have happened?"

"Isn't that rather a morbid thought, John?"

"Perhaps it is. But you understand what I mean. My being there—the top sleuth in all England, as Bobby might romantically conceive me—was a challenge he just couldn't resist. All the way through, he believed he was playing me like a trout in a stream; leading me on to discover and accept the fantastic sham of the case against his uncle."

"He reckoned that the machine, with its substituted tape, was bound to be discovered, and that the case against Charles would then build itself up inexorably?"

"Yes—and he was right in the first supposition, even if he was uncommonly sanguine about the second. The business of the blown fuse was the really tricky part. You see, he had no power to contrive, for the benefit of the passing Friary, what may be called the *real thing*. He couldn't, I mean, have Charles enact the sinister role he'd invented for him: the recorded conversation going on, coming to an end, being succeeded by Charles's coming out of the belvedere, as if straight from talk with Grace, and joining Friary. So Bobby had to invent a hitch in Charles's supposed plan: the unsuspected blown fuse. It can't be said that Bobby Angrave was deficient in ingenuity." Appleby drew the car to the side of the road, and brought it to a halt. "Look," he said.

They had been climbing steadily, and were now looking back over wooded and gently undulating country in the direction of Charne. The house was clearly visible; and it was possible to suppose that a tiny dot, just distinguishable by the naked eye, was the belvedere itself. Behind that, a fine haze of smoke marked the town; and out from this obscurity there seemed to thrust, like reddish tentacles, the roofs of its advancing suburbs.

"I doubt whether it has long to go," Appleby said. "It will become an expensive private school—or an almost equally expensive establishment for young criminals in the making. I hope they won't be told about the associations of that bloody wood."

"It's very strange. Bobby's doing just what he did there remains unthinkable."

"At least a good deal of thinking went to it—on Bobby's own part."

"I've thought of something. Why did he go and play the thing over at five o'clock yesterday afternoon? It must have occurred to him that he *might* be overheard —as in fact he was by Friary—and with some awkward consequence."

"Partly, I think, it was just his conceit over again; he couldn't keep away from this thing he'd contrived so cleverly. Partly it was *folie de doute*, like getting up in the middle of the night to make sure you have turned off the gas tap. Would the machine play back properly, when eventually it was discovered? So he tested it once more, before putting in the blown fuse. The discovery that Friary had been within earshot must have been a nasty shock to him."

"The whole thing can't really be called clever."

"Of course not. It was precisely lacking in what Bobby believed that he himself set store by."

"Rationality?"

"Just that. That excellent fellow Morrison remarked to me at one point that it's lucky people don't get round to murdering one another all that frequently. It's just too easy. Bobby could have drowned his aunt without leaving the faintest mark on her, so that no suspicion was occasioned. In contriving the signs of possible violence, he was already passing from calculated crime to fantasy. Even as it was, if he had simply gone on to kill Charles exactly as he did, it would probably have been impossible to bring the crime home to him. We'd have tried to make a case, because the sudden disfavour into which the revelation of his drug-peddling had brought him enormously increased his motive. But it's my guess we'd have got nowhere. It was the elaboration of his plan that dished him."

"He must have enjoyed risks for their own sake."

"At least he enjoyed bringing things off. Getting Grace into the wood by herself last night, keeping Charles away, reckoning on that dash of Charles's to the telephone in his office: in all these things he was gambling like mad."

The car was in motion again, and presently Appleby swung it out on the high road and pressed the accelerator.

"*Like* mad?" Judith said. "He *was* mad."

"Perhaps so. Perhaps it's charitable to say that his plan was even madder than it was wicked. But the only dispassionate verdict is that Bobby Angrave was too pleased with his own cleverness, poor young devil."

"John, he was a double murderer—and of people to whom he owed a great deal. He had no future in society whatever. But ought you to have let him get out of the music room, grab that shotgun, and kill himself?"

"Morrison certainly didn't think so. He has a feeling that the conclusion of the affair reflects on the efficiency of his men. But in the end he spoke to me very decently. He's a good chap."

"You haven't answered my question, have you? Ought you to have let Bobby take that way out?"

"In my public character—obviously not." The accelerator went down a little further. Charne was being left behind at a speed only short of the dangerous. "And as for the private man—well, there are questions it is useless to ask oneself."